At Issue

| Celebrities in Politics

Other Books in the At Issue Series

At Issue

| Celebrities in Politics

Lisa Idzikowski, Book Editor

GREENHAVEN
PUBLISHING

Published in 2020 by Greenhaven Publishing, LLC
353 3rd Avenue, Suite 255, New York, NY 10010

Cover image: Drew Angerer/Getty Images

Library of Congress Cataloging-in-Publication Data

Names: Idzikowski, Lisa, editor.
Title: Celebrities in politics / Lisa Idzikowski, book editor.
Description: First edition. | New York : Greenhaven Publishing, 2020. |
  Series: At issue | Includes bibliographical references and index. |
  Audience: Grade 9 to 12.
Identifiers: LCCN 2018061360| ISBN 9781534505186 (library bound) | ISBN
  9781534505193 (pbk.)
Subjects: LCSH: Mass media—Political aspects—United States—Juvenile
  literature. | Celebrities—Political activity—United States—Juvenile
  literature. | Motion picture actors and actresses—Political
  activity—United States—Juvenile literature. | Political culture—United
  States—Juvenile literature.
Classification: LCC P95.82.U6 C45 2020 | DDC 306.2—dc23
LC record available at https://lccn.loc.gov/2018061360

Manufactured in the United States of America

Website: http://greenhavenpublishing.com

Contents

Introduction

Entertainers, professional athletes, musicians, actors, comedians, and singers—one of these probably comes to mind when one thinks of a celebrity. Many people enjoy watching professional sports, movies, and television shows for entertainment or relaxation. But does viewing go beyond simple entertainment? Do the celebrities—the athletes, actors, musical artists, and entertainers—have influence over people in their audience? Do audience members either knowingly or unknowingly allow the celebrities to possess this influence over them? This phenomenon may be significant. A Rasmussen Report poll in 2017 relates that 79% of American adults believe that others in the US pay too much attention to celebrities instead of news that really matters.[1]

Without a doubt, professional athletes and entertainment celebrities influence others. Most parents have experienced this firsthand if their children are involved in organized sports. Many kids emulate their favorite sports stars and see them as role models, and some athletes embrace and deliver on the challenge. The same can also be said of other entertainers.

So where is the controversy? It tends to occur when celebrities become involved in politics. It prompts a number of questions about how far the influence of celebrities should extend. Should celebrities be active in the political sphere? Should celebrities influence others in the area of politics, or even become celebrities themselves? All are worthy of exploration, particularly in a celebrity-centric culture.

But despite how contemporary this issue may seem, celebrities have been involved in politics in many different ways since almost the beginning of the United States. Some authors suggest that even though celebrity status looked different in the era before technology, early military heroes like George Washington and

Davy Crockett—who served in Congress from 1833 to 1835—used their celebrity status for political influence. Through the years, celebrities have openly thrown their support behind the politicians of their choice. Historian Kathryn Cramer Brownell from Purdue University says that President John F. Kennedy "relied on celebrity hype to assert his political credibility as a presidential nominee on the primary trail and then eventually to win the election to the White House" and that he "connected with people as fans first, then as voters second."[2] One of the most well-known and well-loved heartthrobs and singers of the era, Frank Sinatra, openly and eagerly supported Kennedy.

Fast forward to today, with the #MeToo and Time's Up movements taking the US and the world by storm. Many celebrities are involved in both of these political and social movements. Steven Bannon, former chief strategist to President Donald Trump, said in 2018 that Time's Up is "the single most powerful potential political movement in the world."[3] But not everyone agrees that celebrities should put their energy into these venues.

Some question whether celebrities should be involved in politics or speak out about social issues. Proponents argue that it is well within their rights as US citizens. One reason voters want celebrities to be involved in politics, they say, is because politicians (and the people that typically have been involved in politics) have not lived up to their expectations. A Gallup Poll demonstrates this fact and how this disappointment in government has evolved over time. In November of 2018, 74% of Americans disapproved of the job that Congress was doing.[4] Compare that to April of 1974, when only 47% disapproved. It follows that Americans want to vote for someone outside the typical political sphere. They want someone to "drain the swamp," as Donald Trump proclaimed often during his presidential campaign.

Some critics of celebrities as politicians argue that celebrities should quit claiming they're going to run for president, regardless of whether it is a well-known celebrity like Kanye West or Dwayne "The Rock" Johnson, or individuals that have already served in some form of governmental position, like Arnold Schwarzenegger or Jesse "The Body" Ventura (who both served as state governors). Some critics even go so far to say that Ronald Reagan, actor turned fortieth US president, and Donald Trump have no business running the country due to their lack of political experience.

But aside from celebrity politicians, what about celebrities that want to pursue social or humanitarian causes? Should they be vocal or demonstrative? One would be right to guess that there are both critics and proponents of this kind of activism. In the 1960s, well-liked entertainers such as Sammy Davis Jr., Harry Belafonte, Muhammad Ali, and others spoke out strongly for civil rights. By the 1980s, Meryl Streep was testifying before Congress about pesticides in America's food supply.[5] In the past several years a few actors in particular have extended themselves into social campaigns around the world. George Clooney, Oprah Winfrey, and Angelina Jolie stand out among a considerable group of celebrities. Oprah has done much to educate girls in Africa by starting the Oprah Winfrey Leadership Academy for Girls in South Africa, and Jolie has supported many campaigns of humanitarian relief, including in her role as an ambassador to the UN Human Rights Commission. However, there are also concerns that celebrities become involved in activism and humanitarian work without fully informing themselves, which can cause more harm than good.

Politically active professional athletes have not stayed on the sidelines either. Perhaps the most publicized and well known is the protest by football quarterback Colin Kaepernick. In 2016, Kaepernick began protesting police brutality and racial injustice during the pre-game playing of the national anthem. At first, he sat on the sidelines. Later his protest morphed into "taking a knee" during the anthem. As the season progressed, other athletes joined in. Not surprisingly, many people did not agree with Kaepernick's demonstration, accusing him of being unpatriotic. Fans ripped up jerseys, booed players, and refused to attend games or watch them on TV, but the protests nonetheless succeeded at giving the issue of racial injustice a new platform.

As these examples demonstrate, the topic of celebrities involved with politics is a controversial and multifaceted issue. As with any controversial topic there are numerous committed proponents, opponents, activists, and experts with worthwhile ideas to share, and the viewpoints in *At Issue: Celebrities in Politics* aim to enable debate and clarification on this important issue.

Notes

1. "Americans See Too Much Celebrity News," *Rasmussen Reports*, November 15, 2017, http://www.rasmussenreports.com/public_content/lifestyle/general_lifestyle/november_2017/americans_see_too_much_celebrity_news.

2. "Historian on JFK's celebrity image—then and now," by Amy Patterson Neubert, *Purdue University News*, November 14, 2013, https://www.purdue.edu/newsroom/releases/2013/Q4/historian-on-jfks-celebrity-image—then-and-now.html.

3. "Bannon Says 'Time's Up Is World's Most Powerful Political Movement," by the Associated Press, *Bloomberg*, September 15, 2018, https://www.bloomberg.com/news/articles/2018-09-15/steve-bannon-time-s-up-is-most-powerful-political-movement.

4. "Congress and the Public," Gallup, https://news.gallup.com/poll/1600/congress-public.aspx.

5. "The Lessons of the Alar Scare," *Chicago Tribune*, June 14, 1989, https://www.chicagotribune.com/news/ct-xpm-1989-06-14-8902090470-story.html.

1

Hollywood Celebrities Are Fighting for the Rights of All Women

Deborah Shaw

Deborah Shaw holds a PhD in Latin American literature and teaches film studies at the University of Portsmouth. She is the co-editor of the Routledge Journal Transnational Cinemas *and the author of* The Three Amigos: The Transnational Filmmaking of Guillermo del Toro, Alejandro González Iñárritu, and Alfonso Cuarón.

Time's Up is a movement that was created by professional women in the entertainment industry. Some wondered if the movement was just a platform for rich celebrities, but Shaw claims this wasn't the case. Evidence supporting this assertion includes the backing of a Latina farm workers' association, which wrote to express their gratitude that celebrities began Time's Up to expose the abuse by individuals in positions of power in various fields. Women from all walks of life and economic circumstances have joined together to push for the end of sexism and harassment.

I t appears that 2018 is already shaping up to be the year of women working together across race and class divides to fight back against sexism and sexual harassment. On the very first day of January, new movement Time's Up was announced via an open letter from women working in the entertainment industry. While it

"Why it's so important that Hollywood's powerful women are standing up for all female workers," by Deborah Shaw, The Conversation, January 4, 2018, https://theconversation.com/why-its-so-important-that-hollywoods-powerful-women-are-standing-up-for-all-female-workers-89661. Licensed under CC BY-ND 4.0.

could have just been a statement against the alleged sexual assault and harassment of those working in Hollywood, this was a message of solidarity to all "sisters."

Some very powerful women in the entertainment industry created Time's Up, but this is not about personal gain—they are using their status to help the disempowered. Time's Up is all about high-profile women using their privilege to highlight and counter sexual discrimination against all women in employment, whatever industry they are in.

The movement is the work of more than 300 female professionals from the fields of television, film and theatre, including producers, actresses, writers and directors. Just a selection of the starry names leading and contributing to the initiative are Emma Stone, Natalie Portman, Cate Blanchett, Ashley Judd, America Ferrera, Rashida Jones, Selena Gomez, Reese Witherspoon, Kerry Washington, Eva Longoria and Ellen Page, as well as Donna Langley, the chairwoman of Universal Pictures, and top lawyers Nina L. Shaw and Tina Tchen. As the days have gone on, more notable women have been publicly adding their names to the campaign and contributing to the fund, too, using the Twitter hashtag #TIMESUP.

Hollywood's feminists have previously been accused of representing an elitist group, who are far removed from the struggles of ordinary, less glamorous women. The Time's Up movement is a serious attempt to counter these accusations through showing solidarity with working women of all backgrounds and ethnicities.

Their aim is to raise $15m for a legal defense fund that can benefit low-income victims of sexual misconduct. They also want to campaign for new legislation to protect women from harassment, and work towards gender parity at studios and talent agencies. A request has also been issued for celebrities to raise awareness by wearing black while walking the red carpet at the Golden Globe awards on January 7.

All Women

The campaign's cross class solidarity was prompted by a letter of support from the predominantly Latina Alianza Nacional de Campesinas. This national female farm workers' organisation wrote to the women of Hollywood who had spoken out against sexual abuse following allegations against Harvey Weinstein and others.

In a moving section of their letter, the farm workers wrote:

> We do not work under bright stage lights or on the big screen. We work in the shadows of society in isolated fields and packinghouses that are out of sight and out of mind for most people in this country. Your job feeds souls, fills hearts and spreads joy. Our job nourishes the nation with the fruits, vegetables and other crops that we plant, pick and pack.
>
> Even though we work in very different environments, we share a common experience of being preyed upon by individuals who have the power to hire, fire, blacklist and otherwise threaten our economic, physical and emotional security.

While the farm workers might be expected to level accusations of elitism against their wealthy sisters, they stood with them. Despite the enormous gulf in social and economic status, they offered their support—"Please know that you're not alone. We believe and stand with you."

This act of solidarity clearly touched the entertainment professionals who have, through the Time's Up movement, taken the first concrete steps to support poor working women. The Time's Up letter mirrors the language used by Alianza, while initiatives like the legal defence fund are a clear demonstration that this is more than just a PR exercise:

> To the members of Alianza and farmworker women across the country, we see you, we thank you, and we acknowledge the heavy weight of our common experience of being preyed upon, harassed, and exploited by those who abuse their power and threaten our physical and economic security.

This collective action taken by so many women in the film, television and theatre industries is unprecedented. Using the celebrity status created by the very industry in which they have suffered might just be the best way to seek to protect all women from abuse, harassment and sexism.

2

Celebrities Getting Political: Nothing New About That

Seth Masket

Seth Masket is a political scientist at the University of Denver and a contributing writer to Pacific Standard.

There's nothing new about celebrities using their popular appeal to enter politics. In fact, this phenomenon may have started back in the era of military heroes like George Washington and Davy Crockett. Some celebrities like Ronald Reagan or Arnold Schwarzenegger have even made the jump into politics. They did so with a gradual learning curve and apprenticeship in politics, while Donald Trump— the latest celebrity to enter office—vowed to make Washington work like his previous business ventures and has not adhered to traditional political tactics.

The past week has seen more than its usual share of political activism by celebrities. Jimmy Kimmel may have played a key role in undermining the latest attempt by Senate Republicans to repeal the Affordable Care Act. Morgan Freeman is trying to raise concerns about Russian interference into the 2016 presidential election. Donald Trump attacked Colin Kaepernick Friday night, only to get pushback from Steph Curry (who then got disinvited

"When Celebrities Get Political," by Seth Masket, September 26, 2017. First published in *Pacific Standard* and reprinted with permission of Pacific Standard 2018.

from a White House visit) and LeBron James, which escalated into a full-scale war over the weekend between Trump and that bastion of liberalism known as the National Football League.

None of this is occurring out of the blue, of course. Trump himself has publicly courted support from conservative celebrities like Ted Nugent and Scott Baio, and the communications director of the White House Office of Public Liaison is Omarosa Manigault, a person whose primary experience has been appearances on Trump's show *The Apprentice*. We shouldn't overlook that Trump himself is, in many ways, the ultimate celebrity politician. His main career over the past several decades has really been the maintenance of his own name as a brand; he's famous for being famous, and jumped into the presidency without developing any real skills or experience as a politician.

Are we witnessing something new here? Is this the dawn of the era of the celebrity?

In many ways, no. American political history is shot through with celebrity culture and has been so for a very long time. The concept of celebrity was obviously a bit different prior to the development of recorded media and mass entertainment. Military heroes like George Washington, Daniel Boone, and Davy Crockett traded on their fame for political influence in the nation's first century, but arguably military experience is more directly applicable to national politics than acting and singing.

The 20th century saw a great deal of political activism by celebrities. A favorite clip of mine: actor Gary Cooper, testifying as a friendly witness before the House Un-American Activities Committee in 1947 in opposition to communism. He admits he knows little about the subject but thinks it's just not "on the level."

Frank Sinatra performed a campaign song for John F. Kennedy in 1960, just as Rosemary Clooney had done for Adlai Stevenson in 1952. Many entertainers would speak out against the Vietnam War in the late 1960s. Shirley MacLaine was a delegate to the Democratic National Convention in 1972. Richard Nixon openly embraced Elvis Presley and, as my colleague Nancy Wadsworth reminds me, Merle Haggard in an attempt to draw rural white support for his Republican policies. (As California's governor, Ronald Reagan did the same thing when he issued a pardon for Haggard in 1972.)

George H.W. Bush famously tapped Arnold Schwarzenegger to chair the president's Physical Fitness Council, and Bill Clinton ran for president in 1992 with the overt support of Barbra Streisand, Fleetwood Mac, and many other performers. Bono befriended George W. Bush during his lengthy efforts to fight HIV and AIDS. Will.i.am performed a famous campaign song for Barack Obama's 2008 campaign. In the summer of 1990, I interned for the U.S. House Select Committee on Aging, and we brought in Burt Lancaster, then enjoying some late-career fame in the wake of *Field of Dreams* (1989), to testify about Social Security. (He was very charming.)

I could obviously go on. The point is that celebrity political activity, with the encouragement and sometimes overt coordination of politicians, campaigns, and parties, has been quite common for a long time.

Moreover, there's nothing inherently bad about it. Politics is impoverished in many ways when only credentialed people are allowed to participate in it. Yes, we might get a somewhat more substantive take on national politics if Nancy Pelosi and Paul Ryan co-hosted a variety show every weeknight on a major network, but no one would watch it. (OK, I might.) Entertainers have the advantage of being interesting and enjoyable for people to watch, and if they can work some actual useful information into their routines, we may be the better off for it.

In some ways, Kimmel's recent foray into health-care politics was about as good as this sort of thing gets. He was discussing (and, by his own admission, politicizing) his infant son's recent heart surgery, sympathizing with those who do not have his access to health insurance, and getting the facts right on the Graham-Cassidy health-care bill. Obviously not all celebrities approach complex policy matters as deftly or relatably.

What is somewhat different today than in previous examples is Trump himself. He's hardly the first celebrity to run for office, but he did so in an atypical manner. Reagan and Arnold Schwarzenegger, both substantial box office draws before moving into politics, made the transition gradually. Reagan spent years on the lecture circuit honing a vision of modern American conservatism. Schwarzenegger worked on a variety of statewide initiatives and other campaigns. They acknowledged that entertainment and politics were two separate fields, seeking to use successes in the former to help them enter the latter.

Trump had no such, well, apprenticeship. He ran for office essentially saying that he would make Washington work the way he had made other business ventures work, through bullying and cajoling people into deals and keeping people amused. This particular celebrity has shown much less success thus far in either accruing many political accomplishments or getting people to like him. He has demonstrated no more knowledge of policy or deeper understanding of the political system and its norms than he did when he first announced his candidacy for president over two years ago.

Celebrities who dabble in politics usually either become more knowledgeable about the subject over time or just withdraw from it. Trump, ever the trailblazer, is pursuing a different path, remaining simultaneously ignorant and deeply involved.

3

Do Celebrity Endorsements Make a Difference in US Presidential Elections?

Nives Zubcevic-Basic

Dr. Nives Zubcevic-Basic is a senior lecturer at Swinburne University of Technology in Australia. She is the director of the Master of Marketing program and is in the faculty of business and law. Her research focuses on marketing communication and consumer neuroscience.

Do celebrity endorsements make a difference when it comes to presidential campaigns? One thing is for certain: this type of celebrity involvement has been going on for many election cycles. The 2016 election was no exception, but what may be different is the social media element. Celebrities often have a large number of followers on social media sites. Research has shown that some celebrities have a greater influence on the public, and with the right celebrity endorsements, politicians can enjoy political gains.

Celebrities are always part of the show in the US presidential election. This is by no means a new trend. Historians have traced the role of celebrities in politics back to the 1920 election, when Warren Harding was endorsed by film stars including Lillian Russell.

In 1960, John F. Kennedy was endorsed by Rat Pack members Sammy Davis Junior and Dean Martin. More recently, Oprah Winfrey, George Clooney, Will.i.am, Brad Pitt and Samuel L. Jackson supported Barack Obama. Actor Clint Eastwood, however, endorsed Republicans John McCain in 2008 and Donald Trump this time around.

The 2016 election is no different. So how much of a difference, if any, do high-profile endorsements make? And to which demographics?

Who's Endorsing Who?

Both Hillary Clinton and Donald Trump have been endorsed by an army of celebrity supporters.

Some of Clinton's high-profile endorsers include LeBron James, Amy Schumer, Katy Perry, Meryl Streep, Jamie Lee Curtis, Lady Gaga, Ellen DeGeneres, Drew Barrymore, George Clooney, Khloe Kardashian, Kerry Washington, Viola Davis, Britney Spears, John Legend, Richard Gere, Salma Hayek, Lena Dunham, Jennifer Lopez, Beyoncé and Snoop Dogg.

In contrast, some of Trump's supporters include Azealia Banks, Sarah Palin, Kirstie Alley, Tom Brady, Charlie Sheen, Dennis Rodman, Kid Rock, Mike Tyson, Donnie Wahlberg, Gary Busey, Hulk Hogan, Tim Allen and Chuck Norris.

If we simply look at the Twitter power behind some of the celebrities listed above, Clinton's camp—with DeGeneres, Spears, James, Lopez and Beyoncé—has a combined 195.6 million followers, compared to Trump's camp—Sheen, Tyson, Palin, Hogan and Alley—with a combined 21 million followers.

Celebrities often go beyond simple endorsements and make powerful statements such as Elizabeth Banks' "Fight Song" or the star-studded Avengers cast's oblique but powerful statement against Trump.

Celebrities Sell

Advertisements featuring celebrities are a popular marketing strategy. In fact, one in five ads globally features a celebrity. Undoubtedly, endorsements are big business.

Some well-known campaigns include Beyoncé and Pepsi (worth US$50 million), Justin Bieber and OPI nail polish ($12.5 million) and Brad Pitt and Chanel No. 5 ($6.7 million).

Marketers happily spend millions on celebrity endorsers as they are able to leverage "secondary brand associations"—that is, people transfer their opinions and feelings about a celebrity to the brand.

In a cluttered world where myriad messages fight for the attention of time-starved consumers, celebrity endorsers serve as arbiters of public opinion. And so, marketing organisations rely on symbolic and emotional features to generate "sociopsychological associations." Some celebrities are seen to be so aspirational that even a glimpse of them in an ad conveys positive meaning, like athletes Cristiano Ronaldo and Roger Federer.

It's important to understand the traits a celebrity, also referred to as a source, should have in order to transfer positive meaning to a brand. These are broken down into three categories:

- source attractiveness (physique, intellect, athleticism, lifestyle);
- source credibility (expertise, trustworthiness); and
- meaning transfer (compatibility between brand and celebrity).

Quite often, celebrities use their high profile to encourage people, world organisations and politicians to support their cause, like singer Bono's One campaign against poverty. Actors Jack Black and Neil Patrick Harris encouraged Californians to vote against the California Marriage Protection Act.

Not-for-profit and world organisations are aware of the power of celebrities and create connections in order to garner publicity, awareness and donations. This includes the United Nations and Angelina Jolie, and DeGeneres and the Ice Bucket Challenge.

Celebrity Endorsements in Politics Makes Sense

We know celebrities grab and hold consumer attention. They also improve ad recall. People are more likely to think positively about a product because they are familiar with the celebrity.

However, expertise is an important element when wanting to influence consumers. Credibility is another crucial factor that tells us not all celebrities are equal. Those considered to be more credible have a higher influence on people's opinions and decisions.

Celebrities with prior political activism, like Martin Sheen and George Clooney, are more likely to have a stronger influence. Interestingly, people consider celebrities to be more credible and trustworthy than politicians.

A negative comment by a credible endorser such as Oprah Winfrey can be as damaging as a positive one. For example, Winfrey stopped eating burgers during the 1996 "mad cow" spread—this resulted in a 10% drop in cattle futures the next day.

Effectiveness and Audience

Research has found that young adults are more likely to listen to family and friends, rather than celebrities, as a source of political information.

At the same time, young people believe celebrities have an effect on the way people think—more than politicians, scientists or academics. Outside of age, ethnicity and gender are also known to affect celebrity endorsement influence.

For instance, African-American and Caucasian-American voters are more likely to rely on family and friends. However, Asian-American, Polynesian and Hispanic voters are more likely to trust politicians or interest groups. Also, men consider celebrities to have a greater influence than women do, regardless of cultural background.

Celebrities are able to motivate young people to seek further information and to take part. However, this is less true of first-time voters. Those who are less politically savvy or poorly informed are also more likely to vote for a political party endorsed by a celebrity.

What's interesting is that most celebrities tend to align themselves with politically uncontroversial issues and tend to steer towards liberal perspectives—for example, George Clooney and Not On Our Watch, a campaign for improving human rights.

Trump's camp includes controversial celebrities who have previously been involved in controversial branding endorsements, like Charlie Sheen and underwear brand Hanes.

Trump was also a celebrity prior to becoming a candidate. People's experience of his public persona through his roles on TV have over time instilled a specific meaning. That meaning is now transferred to his political campaign.

So What's the Final Verdict?

With the right celebrity endorsements, political campaigns can do quite well.

Oprah Winfrey's endorsement of Obama in 2008 was found to increase overall voter participation and number of contributions received by Obama, and an estimated overall 1 million additional votes.

All it takes is trustworthiness, credibility, and a lot of followers.

4

The Early Days of Celebrities and Politics

Brian Cowan

Brian Cowan teaches in the department of history and classical studies at McGill University. He is an associate of the Multigraph Collective which has produced the title Interacting with Print: Element of Reading in the Era of Print Saturation, *published by University of Chicago Press.*

What came first: celebrities or politics? Turns out that in the past, the way to become a celebrity was through politics. In England, individuals became well known as a result of being persecuted in some way, often because of religious beliefs that went against the political establishment. Flash forward to Barack Obama, who worked to maintain a public persona that was as amiable as modern film stars and fluent in social media. Some political pundits say that to win in future elections, candidates will have to be well-known celebrities, and while the means of catching the public's attention have changed, the element of theatricality in politics is an enduring aspect.

D onald Trump's surprising victory in the 2016 US Presidential election demonstrated that celebrity is now a political force to be reckoned with. Famous actors such as Ronald Reagan or Arnold Schwarzenegger have held high office in the past in the US, and Indian film stars such as Jayalalithaa Jayaram or Maruthur Gopalan Ramachandran (popularly known as MGR) translated

"Celebrity and politics before Trump," by Brian Cowan, Oxford University Press, December 8, 2016. Reprinted by permission.

their fame into successful political careers, but Trump's victory reveals the power of celebrity name recognition as a force for political mobilization, and has highlighted the theatrical aspects of political performance in our heavily mediated society. Trump's success has already encouraged other celebrities such as Kanye West and Dwayne "The Rock" Johnson to consider making their own presidential bids in the 2020 election. Pundits such as Michael Moore have suggested that the Democratic Party should support a celebrity candidate such as Tom Hanks or Oprah Winfrey as their standard bearer in the future if it wants to find its way back to electoral success.

It would seem that this mix of celebrity culture and politics is a relatively new phenomenon, and indeed celebrity itself is often thought to be something distinctly modern. It's true that the word "celebrity" didn't refer to a particular person until around the mid-nineteenth century, and "celebrity" didn't refer to the experience of fame or popular renown until the later eighteenth century. The French historian Antoine Lilti has referred to celebrity as "a radically new form of renown." It's easy to understand why one might think that celebrity has only gradually become a politically potent currency.

But there were celebrities long before that particular word identified them as such, and there was a time when politics made celebrities rather than the other way around. Before the later eighteenth century, the word 'celebrity' tended to refer to ceremony. Celebrity was a way of describing the pomp and circumstance that traditionally accompanied important public rituals such as weddings, funerals, and royal processions. Celebrity was intricately linked to the magic, charm, and charisma associated with the church and royalty, and this meant that celebrity was inherently political—contemporary fame was produced by the majesty of royal or spiritual power, or preferably both. It's important to understand this connection between premodern, ceremonial forms of fame, and their modern successors known as celebrities.

Modern celebrity is in many ways a product of the new publics created by the early modern printing revolution. The mass production of words and images enabled by the printing press allowed people to learn about, and recognize, contemporary figures in hitherto unprecedented ways. This early modern media revolution allowed for kings, queens, and religious leaders such as Martin Luther (1483–1546) or the English Protestant martyrs memorialized by John Foxe (1516/17–1587) to become famous with greater speed and extent than had been possible.

The political turmoils of early modern England helped to create new celebrities. The most effective means of turning ordinary people into celebrities was through persecution, and particularly through the spectacle of judicial process. Political trials were full-scale media events in early modern England. John Foxe's *Acts and Monuments* (1563) cultivated an appetite amongst early modern readers for the stories of the tribulations of otherwise ordinary people who were persecuted for their religious beliefs. In the seventeenth century, the stories of people who were prosecuted for political transgressions also garnered a large readership. By the early eighteenth century, these stories would be collected into volumes called *State Trials* (1719) and they would be reprinted, augmented, and further anthologized right through the nineteenth century. Works such as the *State Trials* and Foxe's *Acts and Monuments* served to preserve for posterity the fame of individuals who had gained notoriety through their persecution.

In some cases, judicial persecution could create a political celebrity. The Tory clergyman, Dr. Henry Sacheverell, was impeached in Parliament for high crimes and misdemeanors in 1710 in response to some intemperate and fiery words he had preached at St. Paul's Cathedral. Although Sacheverell was found guilty, his punishment was mercifully light—he was simply banned from preaching for three years and his sermon was ordered to be burned—and so he emerged from the experience as a celebrity and a hero for the Tory cause. Sacheverell became perhaps the best known person in England with the exception of the reigning monarch, Queen Anne, and he even took to imitating monarchical practices such as going on a celebrated progress across the country. Religious and political divisions helped to construct a new celebrity.

Perhaps it is too easy to forget that politics has always been at the heart of celebrity. While some historians of celebrity have been inclined to draw a direct line between the London stage of the eighteenth century through to modern-day Hollywood, it is better to remember that the charisma that is at the heart of celebrity has always been as much about power as well as entertainment.

During his presidency, Barack Obama has sometimes been referred to as "the first celebrity president" in which he remodeled the presidency in ways that were more suited to twenty-first century forms of communication, such as social media, and his careful construction of a public persona that resembled likeable film stars more so than aloof policy wonks. While the juxtaposition of the presentation of personality for public entertainment as well as for political leadership has sometimes seemed awkward, theatricality and politics have always been closely related. The election of a former reality TV star to the office of President of the United States of America is less surprising than it might otherwise seem if we recognize the importance of attention grabbing and performance skills are to a highly mediated political culture such as our own.

5

Voters in the US Like the Idea of Celebrities Running for Office

Natalie Zarrelli

Natalie Zarrelli is a frequent contributor to the online journal Atlas Obscura. Zarelli writes about history and science, especially involving women.

Americans like celebrities not only for their role in entertainment but also as potential politicians. It is a known fact that many in the US don't believe that career politicians act appropriately, so it is no surprise that celebrities interested in running for political office are accepted as alternatives by many Americans. Celebrities have characteristics that give them an advantage in politics: they are good at acting, they are political outsiders, and people accept faults in celebrities that they wouldn't in traditional politicians.

It seems like a millennium has passed since Donald Trump announced he was running for President in June 2015. Now the businessman is president-elect, with the U.S. split between celebrating, protesting, and drifting into a black hole of nihilistic depression. Clearly, the reasons why Trump resonated with so many American voters are complex. But one of the Republican candidate's main draws, throughout the campaign, has been his celebrity and outsider status.

"Why Americans Consider Celebrities for Political Office," by Natalie Zarrelli, Atlas Obscura, November 10, 2016. Reprinted by permission.

Before 2015, most people recognized Trump best from the reality show *The Apprentice* or his antics on the WWE; sixteen years ago, his candidacy was a fly-by joke on The Simpsons. When former first lady Barbara Bush labeled Trump more of a "comedian or a showman" than a politician, it was not seen as a compliment. Yet Trump's lack of political experience is something he and his supporters frequently cite as an asset, so it's worth examining the celebrity-politician phenomenon.

Trump joins stars like Arnold Schwarzenegger, Ronald Reagan, Clint Eastwood, Sonny Bono, and Shirley Temple Black in making a successful turn to politics. But while a dearth of previous political involvement would normally hurt a candidate's chances, in the case of celebrities it seems not to matter much. So why *do* people embrace celebrities running for political office? And what are the pros and cons of starting out in Hollywood, and going on to influence legislation?

Well, at a time when only 16 percent of Americans think the government does the right thing "most of the time," celebrities might be viewed less negatively than politicians are, says Robert Erikson, Professor of Political Science at Columbia University. Some stars may feel like a known quantity to voters already—even if their stances on various positions are unknown.

Many campaigns begin by telling the public their story of who the candidate is, something celebrities don't really need to do. And most of the time, people vote along party lines, rather than for a specific politician, according to Joshua Tucker, Professor of Political Science at NYU. "Most of the votes for offices on the ballot besides president, and maybe governor, senator, and representative—most people have never heard of any of those people, so they just default to party," Tucker says. Perhaps unsurprisingly, voters the world over tend to be more responsive to candidates they are familiar with.

But it's not just that. "Actors can be good at acting and that is a requirement of politics. Reagan was successful playing the role of president," says Erikson. "Celebrities can have more experience and talent in front of audiences than politicians," he adds. "See Trump as an example." These on-camera talents can help them navigate scandals more deftly than normal politicians might, since the public may view drama as part of a celebrity's personal brand.

Ronald Reagan, elected in 1980, became president after acting in Hollywood for nearly 30 years. "As president, Reagan combined a masterful use of television and radio with a great sense of pseudo–event theatrics," West and Orman write. "Indeed, he threw himself into the role of president as much as he worked himself up for the role of George Gipp in the *Knute Rockne* movie. Reagan became an outstanding performer in the drama of national political life."

In the book *Celebrity Politics*, Darryl M. West and John M. Orman point out that celebrities aren't far from politics to begin with; politicians are often endorsed by celebrities. When voters don't know what a politician stands for, they look to trusted guides—which include celebrities. Indeed, there isn't much difference between the way the public sees politicians and entertainers, says professor Benjamin Bishin of the University of California, however different they may be. We often view our political leaders through the same mediums where we get our entertainment, which mixes our perceptions of them.

When a candidate is shifting their arena from entertainment to politics, advertising their lack of political credentials is often "a choice the candidate is making in trying to frame his or her appeal," says Tucker. "A candidate like [former Minnesota Governor Jesse] Ventura or Trump, however, can also try to appeal to people who want someone "outside the system" to "shake things up."

In 1998, when Jesse Ventura left his tie-dyed spandex pants behind him at World Wrestling Entertainment and ran for the Mayor of Minnesota, his campaign ads featured him as an action figure, wearing a suit. As two kids played with the toy, a voice announced: "You can make Jesse battle special interest groups!"

and "Don't waste your money on politics as usual!" Far from ignoring his wrestling past, Ventura wanted Minnesotans to take the metaphor of fighting in the ring to fighting for policy.

"Voters often prefer an outsider who can either promise to fight corruption, or who will promise to overcome partisan division and fix things," Bishin says."This is an always unmet promise of being post-partisan." Arnold Schwarzenegger, while distancing himself from his roles in action movies like *Terminator*, asserted in campaign ads for Governor of California (which he won in 2003) that "politicians are not doing their job." He promised to "bring California back again."

While scandals are often the ruin of politicians' careers, we expect celebrities to have faults and marry multiple times; when they smash through glass doors with their bare hands in a drunken stupor, we shake our heads. But politicians are held to a different standard. "The 'dirt' on Trump has not harmed him as much as one might think," Erikson says. "I cannot imagine a politician bragging like he did with Billy Bush and the women coming forward." While he adds that Bill Clinton was a popular president when his own scandals were revealed, "an ordinary politician—say a middle-aged senator with a family—could not have gotten away with it."

Celebrities are drawn to both of America's major political parties, but sometimes circumstances drive a party to look for candidates in unlikely places, particularly if they're lacking a ready pool of politicians looking to advance their careers. "I have noticed for instance that Republicans often tap local TV newscasters or even weathermen as candidates for office. They are celebrities at the local level," Erikson says.

There are definite benefits to being a celebrity when going into politics, but it doesn't guarantee success. "The bigger disadvantage would be in not knowing how to be effective as a politician," says Tucker. He explains that in a presidential election, politicians know it will become a two-candidate race, and it's the norm for most politicians to reframe their campaign toward the center of the political spectrum to appeal to more voters; celebrities don't necessarily capitalize on this strategy, and sometimes suffer for it.

Jello Biafra, who runs record label Alternative Tentacles and is famous as the lead singer for The Dead Kennedys, ran for mayor of San Francisco in 1979 with the slogan "There's always room for Jello," and ran for president under the Green Party in 2000. But his serious policies, which included elections for police officers (by the people they patrol) and legalized squatting in tax-lapsed buildings, were overshadowed by his punk history and the part of his platform that required businessmen to wear clown suits. Biafra later became involved in campaigns for Ralph Nader and Gore, and still engages in political discussion on YouTube.

Debates, Tucker says, can also be a problem for people who weren't trained to handle them. While Trump's celebrity background might have helped him during the primaries when he was interacting with others onstage, "he certainly looked inexperienced when compared to Clinton in the one-on-one general election debates," Tucker says. "I doubt a polished politician would have walked around on stage, for example, the way Trump did in the second debate."

When celebrities do manage to learn the ins and outs of politics, though, their fans show their support. Shirley Temple Black, who became a foreign ambassador, told the New York Times in 1989 that "Shirley Temple opens doors for Shirley Temple Black." Ben Jones, who was famous for his role on *The Dukes of Hazard* and later served two terms as a Democratic congressman of Georgia, said in an interview that, "It's a funny thing, I was sort of the last guy you would think to run for Congress and it turned out I had a knack for it."

The 2016 election has arguably been the most anxiety-infused political event in recent history. Noting how we vote and why is as important as ever, as it's likely that we'll see more celebrities running for political office. We won't know for a while which scripts they'll be following, though. With his divisive rhetoric, Trump seems to have tossed the blueprints for both normal politicians and celebrity candidates out the window.

Actor and writer Orson Welles once pointed out that the two professions are two sides to the same bizarre coin. "I don't think [politicians] are crooks; I think they are actors," said Welles. "But that kind of acting is not lying, as long as it refers to and reflects and exhausts the essential commonly held ideals of a culture. Those performances are part of our culture even though they are performances."

6

Does the First Amendment Protect Political Protest by Celebrities?

Shontavia Johnson

Shontavia Johnson is Associate Vice President at Clemson University and is a tenured professor in the department of sociology, anthropology, and criminal justice. Johnson is a frequent contributor to the online news site the Conversation.

Celebrities use their fame to endorse many products and companies reap the benefits, and in the same vein many celebrities also seek to sway the minds of fans in the political arena. Social movements in America, such as women's suffrage and the civil rights movement, have had their share of celebrities speaking and acting in their favor. More recently, sports figures have put their political opinions out there. It is well known that many people are highly motivated by the actions and opinions of celebrities, but does the first amendment protect all of this political activism? What it doesn't protect are actions or speech forbidden by private employers, which can also affect celebrities.

W hen NFL player Colin Kaepernick refuses to stand for the national anthem, or the cast of the Broadway musical *Hamilton* confronts the vice president-elect, or the Dixie Chicks speak out against war, talk quickly turns to freedom of speech.

"Celebrity voices are powerful, but does the First Amendment let them say anything they want?" by Shontavia Johnson, The Conversation, December 12, 2016. https://theconversation.com/celebrity-voices-are-powerful-but-does-the-first-amendment-let-them-say-anything-they-want-69467. Licensed under CC BY-ND 4.0 International.

Most Americans assume they have a constitutional guarantee to express themselves as they wish, on whatever topics they wish. But how protected by the First Amendment are public figures when they engage in political protest?

Coming out publicly, whether for or against some disputed position, can have real consequences for the movement and the celebrity. However helpful a high-profile endorsement may be at shifting the public conversation, taking these public positions—particularly unpopular ones—may not be as protected as we assume. As a professor who studies the intersection of law and culture, I believe Americans may need to revisit their understanding of U.S. history and the First Amendment.

Harnessing the Power of Celebrity

Far from being just product endorsers, celebrities can and do use their voices to influence policy and politics. For example, some researchers believe Oprah Winfrey's early endorsement of Barack Obama helped him obtain the votes he needed to become the 2008 Democratic nominee for president.

This phenomenon, however, is not new.

Since the birth of the nation, celebrities have used their voices—and had their voices used—to advance important causes. In 1780, George Washington enlisted the help of Marquis de Lafayette, a French aristocrat dubbed by some "America's first celebrity," to ask French officials for more support for the Continental Army. Lafayette was so popular that when he traveled to America some years later, the press reported on each day and detail of his yearlong visit.

Social movements also have harnessed the power of celebrity influence throughout American history. In the early 1900s, after the National Woman Suffrage Association was founded to pursue the right of women to vote, the group used celebrities to raise awareness of the cause. Popular actresses like Mary Shaw, Lillian Russell and Fola La Follette, for example, brought attention to the movement, combining their work with political activism to push the women's suffrage message.

Celeb Actions Can Move the Needle

The civil rights movement of the 1960s benefited from celebrities' actions. For instance, after Sammy Davis Jr., a black comedian, refused to perform in segregated venues, many clubs in Las Vegas and Miami became integrated. Others—including Ossie Davis and Ruby Dee, Dick Gregory, Harry Belafonte, Jackie Robinson and Muhammad Ali—were instrumental in the success of the movement and passage of the Civil Rights Act of 1964. These actors planned and attended rallies, performed in and organized fundraising efforts and worked to open opportunities for other black people in the entertainment industry.

By the 1980s, you could watch Charlton Heston and Paul Newman debate national defense policy and a potential nuclear weapons freeze on television. Meryl Streep spoke before Congress against the use of pesticides in foods. Ed Asner and Charlton Heston publicly feuded about their differing opinions of the Reagan administration's support of right-wing Nicaraguan militant groups.

Whatever you think of how well thought out their opinions are (or aren't), celebrities have the ability to draw attention to social issues in a way others do not. Their large platforms through film, music, sports and other media provide significant amplification for the initiatives they support.

There is, in particular, a measurable connection between celebrity opinions and young people. Most marketing research shows that celebrity endorsements can improve the likelihood that young consumers will choose the endorsed product.

Antagonism Toward Celebrity Activism

Celebrities have been important partners, strategists, fundraisers and spokespeople for social movements and politicians since the earliest days of modern America. Recently, however, celebrities speaking out about policy and politics have received some harsh responses.

Kaepernick, in particular, has received scathing criticism. Fans of his team have burned his jersey in effigy. Mike Evans, another NFL player, drew so much criticism for sitting in protest of Donald Trump's election to the presidency that he was forced to apologize and say he would never do it again. #BoycottHamilton trended on Twitter after the cast of the Broadway show *Hamilton* addressed Mike Pence.

President-elect Donald Trump jumped into the fray, tweeting that he does not support the public expression of sentiments like those of the *Hamilton* cast.

Unprotected Speech

All of this raises significant questions about speech, protests and the law. Often celebrities, commentators and pundits talk about being able to say whatever they want thanks to their right to freedom of speech. But this idea is based on common misconceptions about what the U.S. Constitution actually says.

What is allowed under the law starts with the text of the First Amendment, which provides that:

> *"Congress shall make no law respecting an establishment of religion, or prohibiting the free exercise thereof; or abridging the freedom of speech, or of the press; or the right of the people peaceably to assemble, and to petition the Government for a redress of grievances."*

The language essentially allows for freedom of expression without government interference. The right to free speech includes protests and distasteful speech that one might find offensive or racist.

But, the First Amendment as written applies only to actions by Congress, and by extension the federal government. Over time, it's also come to apply to state and local governments. It's basically a restriction on how the government can limit citizens' speech.

The First Amendment does not, however, apply to nongovernment entities. So private companies—professional sports organizations or theater companies, for instance—can actually restrict speech without violating the First Amendment, because in most cases, it doesn't apply to them (unless the restriction is illegal for other reasons). This is why the NFL could ban DeAngelo Williams from wearing pink during a game in honor of his mother, who had died from breast cancer, and fine him thousands of dollars when he later defied the rules and did it anyway.

How does all of this affect celebrities? In a nutshell, if a celebrity is an employee of, or has some kind of contract with, a nongovernment entity, his speech actually can be restricted in many ways. Remember, it's not against the law for a nongovernment employer to limit what employees can say in many cases. While there are other more limited protections based on state and federal law that protect employee speech, they are incomplete and probably wouldn't apply to most celebrity speech. Any questions about what a public figure can or cannot express, therefore, will start with the language of any contracts she has signed—not the First Amendment.

For better or worse, celebrities can make significant impacts on policy, politics and culture, and have been doing so for centuries. But speaking out can put them at risk. Celebrities can be fined by their employers, like DeAngelo Williams, have their careers derailed, like the Dixie Chicks, or receive death threats, like Colin Kaepernick. Even so, their involvement can provide an influential platform in promoting and creating societal change.

7

Hip-Hop and Politics: The Interplay Between Rap and Political Discourse

Murray Forman

Murray Forman is an associate professor of communications studies at Northeastern University in Boston, Massachusetts. His research focuses on critical analysis of media industries, cultural production and communication, hip-hop, race and identity, and social uses of popular music.

Conscious rap—or rap music that is socially aware and connected to the greater history of public protest—is not a new concept. In fact, it has existed since the dawn of hip-hop, and harkens back to the political-cultural output of the 1960s and 1970s. It has long played a role in articulating political and social issues and galvanizing young people into political action, but this became especially notable leading up to Barack Obama's election as president in 2008. Forman examines the role hip-hop artists and celebrities played in Obama's election as well as their larger role in racial discourse and other political issues.

This article identifies a particular aspect of hip-hop's range of cultural production—conscious rap—in order to isolate one of the more politicized discursive options available to youth in America and a site where critical perspectives on post-Civil

"Conscious Hip-Hop, Change, and the Obama Era," by Murray Forman, American Studies Journal, 2010, http://www.asjournal.org/54-2010/conscious-hip-hop/. Licensed under CC BY-SA 3.0.

Rights America have emerged most forcefully. It further suggests that Obama's political rise corresponds with a new phase in hip-hop and has impacted the ways in which its creative artists frame and articulate issues of race, class, and identity.

In 2002, media and hip-hop scholar Todd Boyd wrote, "we cannot live in the past forever. Civil rights had its day; now it is time to move out of the way" (Boyd, 2002: 152). Six years later, during the 2008 U.S. presidential election year, Double O (of the rap group Kidz in the Hall) declared, "I think hip-hop culture has helped a younger generation see race in a slightly different perspective" (Hale, 2008: 64). These statements, each uttered under different conditions and in separate contexts, ultimately address a transitional phase and a new emergent sensibility pertaining to cultural politics in the United States. For many, U.S. President Barack Obama's 2008 campaign and subsequent election signal a decisive break from the Civil Rights era, providing a crucial moment in the transformation of the nation's discourse around race, culture, and identity. As I endeavor to explain, for all the talk about America entering a "post-racial society," race remains a central issue in American social debates and hip-hop often provides some of the most convincing articulations of its continuing resonance in American cultural politics.

[…]

On Message: Hip-Hop and Conscious Rap

In still other contexts there is a pronounced commitment to cultural themes and an overt politicized discourse that poses an analytical critique of social issues and concerns, especially those that impact the economically or racially disenfranchised citizenry and the nation's black communities in particular. This latter frame, alternately referred to as "message rap" (following the release of the 1982 recording "The Message" by Grandmaster Flash and the Furious Five) or, more commonly, "conscious hip-hop," suggests reflection on and intellectual engagement with pressing social issues (most often involving themes of racial and class struggle). As Michael Eric Dyson explains, conscious rap is "rap that is socially aware and consciously connected to historic patterns of political protest and aligned with progressive forces of social critique" (Dyson, 2007: 64).

Dyson's explicit reference to historical patterns is pertinent since the conscious rap subgenre owes a clear debt to established forms of political-artistic expression of the 1960s and 1970s (including the work of the Black Arts Movement and music by artists such as the Last Poets or Watts Prophets). Indeed, most so-called conscious rap artists are extremely aware of the legacy they uphold and of their connections to previous periods in African-American political struggle and aesthetic innovation. Yet conscious rap also functions in ways that are highly responsive to contemporary socio-political contexts and conditions, aligning it with various community interests *and* artistic strategies *now*. Thus, while the music of hip-hop serves as a powerful means of articulating complex social issues, it must also be understood as just one facet within a much wider system of cultural practices through which political ideologies are processed and proposed in immediate and urgent contexts.

Although hip-hop has always demonstrated a capacity for articulating serious social issues and amplifying critical perspectives on negative conditions that inordinately impact the African-American population, the political nature of the conscious rap subgenre is often deemed unsuitable to commercial interests despite the sales and tour successes of such unambiguously politicized hip-hop acts as Public Enemy.[1] Through the 1980s and early 1990s major record labels were often resistant to signing explicitly politicized acts, suggesting that either the subject matter was too narrowly concerned with black cultural issues and risked alienating the much larger white consumer market or voicing concern that the incendiary lyrics of conscious political rap acts might draw the ire of conservative cultural watchdogs or politicians and jeopardize the label's reputation.

In one example of the backlash against controversial political content and the aggressive stance of politicized conscious rap artists, the Oakland California MC Paris was dropped from his record label Tommy Boy Records (an independent label with a production and distribution deal with the Warner Brothers corporation) in 1992 due to the content and cover art for his album *Sleeping With the Enemy* that had dark allusions to the assassination of then President George H. Bush. President Bush and Vice President Dan Quayle also explicitly criticized hip-hop MC Ice T in 1992 for his confrontational track "Cop Killer" (a song recorded with his heavy metal band, Body Count, castigating police brutality but which is significantly *not* a hip-hop track), released on the Sire/Warner Brothers label. The incident and label pressure led Ice T to remove the track from subsequent pressings of the album. These and other examples reflect the extent to which hip-hop is capable of tweaking the sensibilities of mainstream America, challenging the cultural status quo and provoking intense social debate.

In several more recent instances, acts including Dead Prez, The Coup, or Immortal Technique expound an unambiguous revolutionary program for radical social change. In their view, hip-hop is a medium of communication that is easily accessible to young audiences and that is well suited to conveying uncompromising critiques of dire social issues.[2] Though not formally associated with an explicitly radical political ideology, MCs including Common, Jean Grae, Medusa, Mos Def, Nas, N.Y.Oil, The Roots, or Talib Kweli are regularly cited for their "conscious" lyrics and their progressive attitudes toward gender relations, black-on-black crime, prison reform and various issues relating to race, class, and hegemonic power relations. Though these artists are rarely signed to major record labels (and consequently lack access to the extensive distribution systems and touring support that accompany such circumstances) they thrive in what is defined as the "underground,"[3] often releasing self-produced music independently and on small black-owned record labels, acquiring airplay on campus-community radio stations or exploiting the digital distribution technologies of the Internet.

Politically engaged artists that employ a critical discourse and social critique are also often weighted with additional responsibilities within hip-hop and the wider black community. They fill a void for many youths that have grown tired or suspicious of long-time career politicians and the limitations of established black leaders. These youths seek new ideas and new leadership that are more in tune with their specific needs and that share the same attitudinal and ideological base especially in relation to pressing issues such as educational reform, enhanced employment or career opportunities, revocation of racial profiling practices and improved police relations, or prison and criminal justice reform. The resultant differences in social demands and political approaches contribute to a sharp-edged generational dissonance and, in many instances, hip-hop's conscious MCs clearly and consistently articulate community concerns, positioning them in the vanguard of social activism. Whether they seek it or not, they are commonly cast as role models or leaders; in rare cases (such as the hip-hop duo, Dead Prez) they embrace this responsibility, accepting an important leadership role in social justice movements (Asante, 2008: 151–69).[4]

Perhaps the most galvanizing event for many hip-hop identified youth in the U.S. over the past decade was the inability of the government (under George W. Bush) to protect the citizens of New Orleans and to alleviate the death and destruction in other areas along the Gulf of Mexico coastline following Hurricane Katrina in August 2005. The government's ineffectiveness was shocking and the nation watched in abject horror as the victims of the tragedy were largely left to fend for themselves in the storm's immediate aftermath. New Orleans is renowned as a vital cultural center and its contributions to American music are many and varied, giving birth to jazz music and zydeco as well as other hybrid musical forms. Since the late 1990s, New Orleans also emerged as a key center of hip-hop production with powerhouse record labels No Limit and Cash Money generating massive sales revenue while drawing attention to the intricacies of existence in the city's wards through rap lyrics and music videos that placed the city front and center.

New Orleans is also a city with a predominant African-American population; the 2000 census placed the city's black population at just over 67%. As the devastation of Katrina became clear, the media images reinforced the fact that black families were inordinately impacted by the flooding, especially those that lived in the hard-hit Ninth Ward. The first and perhaps most incendiary hip-hop statement on the tragedy emerged quickly, during NBC-TV's live September 2, 2005 telethon broadcast of the Concert for Hurricane Relief when hip-hop MC and producer Kanye West abruptly veered off script, uttering his now-famous line "George Bush doesn't care about black people." Though the statement is almost surely untrue (severe ineptitude and incredibly poor delegation skills do not necessarily amount to indifference or a lack of care), it cut to the core of the issue that black citizens are routinely exposed to unfair and imbalanced treatment within the white-dominated institutional power structures. Subsequent expressions of outrage emerged from hip-hop artists;[5] Mos Def recorded "Katrina Klap (Dollar Day)," a song based on the rhythmic structure of "Nolia Clap" (by New Orleans MC Juvenile). The track and accompanying video constitute an homage to New Orleans and articulate a sharply derisive rebuke of the government's bungling of the tragedy, cleanup, and community revitalization. Juvenile himself also conveyed the imagery of Katrina's aftermath to the hip-hop audience via his video for "Get Ya Hustle On" featuring footage shot in the wreckage of the Ninth Ward.

The critical theme was taken up and circulated widely among black youth and others who are aligned with the hip-hop community as acknowledged in the text accompanying the video *Katrina Knows* (produced by Harvard University's Hip-Hop Archive):

> *Katrina was a wake-up call to the hip-hop generation. And we didn't even know we were asleep! But Katrina Knew. We knew about injustice, racism, class elitism and regional arrogance. We knew we had a president, congress and a country that seemed to be clinging to old school notions of the American dream, where the perfect America was one without cities, diversity and hip-hop. Katrina came with a vengeance and with all the lessons from the past and lessons for the future. It's like the storm knew we were asleep at the wheel.*[6]

While Katrina is described as a "wake up call," it also constitutes a catalyst, motivating hip-hop-identified youth to more directly engage in political activism and social change. After Katrina there was a notable upswing in hip-hop's political rhetoric and an uncompromising discourse of resistance against the failed policies and actions of the Bush government.

"Change We Can Believe In": Hip-Hop and the Obama Campaign

Of the many powerful discourses that emerged in the period leading to the 2008 election, surely none were more resonant than those framed within the ideals of "Change" and "Hope." Two terms of Republican leadership (and the accompanying policies and initiatives it enacted) clearly fatigued the nation's electorate and the reputation of President George W. Bush and his administration was in tatters in the eyes of many hip-hop-identified voters. Senator Barack Obama emerged as a viable leader despite formidable opposition within his own Democratic party and skepticism among a public with concerns about his age and relative inexperience, his lack of political pedigree, and crucially, concerns about his identity as a black man.[7] For many youth voters, these same factors were welcomed as a crucial departure from the narrow perspectives of standard career politicians and the stultifying effects of a "business as usual" approach to policymaking.

Obama's political rise is an impressive achievement by any measure. A junior figure in the Democratic Party, his 2004 speech at the Democratic National Convention (prior to the defeat of the party's presidential candidate, John Kerry of Massachusetts) galvanized the party faithful and caught the attention of the nation's media as well as the rank and file electorate. His elegance, sophistication, intellectual acumen, and rhetorical skills offered a sharp distinction from other politicians in the political arena and his quintessentially American back-story (Obama, 1995; Obama, 2006) endeared him to countless Americans who share various features of his own formation. As an American of mixed race, with black and white ancestry and a foreign and domestic heritage, Obama presents a different face of American politics and a new model of 21st Century leadership, appealing across lines of racial and class difference. According to hip-hop lawyer Wendy Day, "hip-hop has impacted Obama's campaign [...] I believe white folk have been educated about the struggle and the black experience since the early 80s through rap music. I believe this education and increased awareness has reduced racism within this generation to the point of accepting a black president" (Hale, 2008: 64).

Prior to John Kerry's failed electoral bid, hip-hop artists had occasionally rallied around voter registration campaigns in the attempt to mobilize young first-time voters to participate in electoral politics. Hip-Hop impresario P. Diddy initiated Citizen Change with great fanfare in 2004 with the slogan "vote or die" and various organizers (such as the Boston Hip-Hop Summit Youth Voter Registration Event that was launched at the 2004 Democratic National Convention in Boston) also took up the cause at the local grassroots level.[8] The many hip-hop oriented initiatives were lauded yet they also lacked a solid agenda. According to hip-hop organizer Jeff Johnson, "there was very little substance underneath that movement. Vote or Die, but I'm not going to tell you how. Vote or Die, but I'm not going to help you organize" (Jones, 2008: E2). Though many of these organizations were dormant between national elections, by 2008 there was a renewed groundswell of energy and support for the Obama campaign from within the extended hip-hop community and among the nation's college students.

As Obama gained momentum during the 2008 campaign, hip-hop artists emerged in droves as consistent commentators on national politics and the social landscape, offering pithy analyses and expressing an urgent need for change. While Obama's blackness was clearly a factor in their engagement, so, too, was his age. He was generally accepted as a member of the hip-hop generation, having grown and matured in a world with hip-hop; in 1979 when the first major rap recording "Rapper's Delight" (by the Sugarhill Gang) was released, Obama was 18 years old. By the time MTV began airing rap music videos on the program *Yo! MTV Raps* in 1988, he was 27 and during his campaign he openly admitted to enjoying rap music and having music by Jay-Z, Ludacris and others on his iPod[9] and on several occasions different rap artists and hip-hop impresario Russell Simmons accompanied him at public appearances. Obama's musical tastes and his hip-hop endorsements impressed some members of the hip-hop generation but, as Jay-Z notes in the track "Streets is Watching," his detractors were also "Waiting for you to break, make your first mistake, can't ignore it."

Obama's early career work as a community organizer also endeared him to the urban youth constituency. As he describes in detail in his first memoir, he decided in 1983 to "organize black folks. At the grass roots. For change" (Obama, 1995: 133).[10] Obama subsequently worked for two years in Chicago's South Side neighborhoods, home to a sizable African-American, Latino and immigrant population and a region renowned for its urban poverty and accompanying problems. This experience reinforced his sense of service and deeply influenced his sense of commitment to disenfranchised urban citizens, further aligning him with their sensibilities, frustrations and dreams. As his reflections indicate, he clearly comprehends many of the vital issues and conditions that influence those youth that are most deeply immersed in hip-hop's discourses and cultural practices. There was widespread acceptance of Obama's candidacy among urban youths that have been marginalized or vilified within American social institutions—especially the education system and areas related to criminal justice and the nation's penal system and labor and employment. Phonte Coleman of the group Little Brother confirms this relationship with his comment, "I just think we're excited about the possibility of a president who really understands what it's like to be us" (Hale, 2008).

It was not only rap artists and entrepreneurs that emerged in the political arena during the 2008 campaign. New York hip-hop activist Rosa Clemente ran as the vice-presidential candidate on the national Green Party ticket and Kevin Powell, a longtime hip-hop commentator and slam-poetry artist ran for a seat in the U.S. Congress. In Newark, New Jersey mayor Cory Booker, in his 30s, navigated traditional political establishment circles as well as sites more commonly associated with the city's hip-hop oriented youth scene, effectively bridging an ideological gap that has at times caused tension between different age constituencies (Boyd, 2002; Nuruddin, 2004: 272-273). The evidence suggests that the hip-hop generation is now coming of age and as they do, they are accepting new service responsibilities, taking up the baton of political leadership that has been passed (or wrested from) old-guard political leaders.

Obama's suave and confident image, along with the campaign slogans "hope" and "change," was rapidly disseminated in and through the hip-hop apparatus. The iconic blue and red image produced by graphic artist Shepard Fairey was adopted as a national symbol of hope among Democratic supporters, eventually reaching the Smithsonian Institution's National Portrait Gallery where it joined other estimable paintings of American presidents. Fairey's aesthetic pedigree is itself formed within a convergence of punk and hip-hop influences; his willful appropriation (some define it as a matter of outright plagiarism[11]) of media images reflects rap music's cut'n'mix or sampling processes and his predilection for postering urban spaces corresponds with hip-hop's graffiti pieces. As an indication of the reach and resonance of Fairey's Obama visage, the image was widely appropriated among hip-hop producers, emerging in numerous other hip-hop contexts including t-shirts, posters and CD covers.

Several rap artists specifically incorporated Obama's voice and utterances into their recordings in 2008 prior to the national election. For example, Will.i.am of the group Black Eyed Peas produced the Emmy Award-winning video "Yes We Can" which circulated widely via YouTube. The song features musicians, actors, and sports celebrities singing in unison with Obama's spoken words, including the line, "nothing can stand in the way of the power of millions of voices calling for change," accompanied by the graphic display of the words "change," "hope" and "vote." In another case, employing the hook from Tupac Shakur's posthumous 1998 release "Changes,"[12] Queens New York MC Nas builds the 2008 track "Black President" around vocal interpolations sampled from Obama's January 3, 2008 Iowa state caucus victory ("they said this day would never come") and his April 19, 2008 speech in Harrisburg, PA ("we will change the world").

"Black President" is clearly intended as a tribute and an endorsement with the lines, "On a positive side/I think Obama provides hope and challenges minds/of all races and colors to erase the hate/and try to love one another, so many political snakes." Yet while Nas celebrates the ascent of the first truly viable African-American presidential candidate and the possibility of a new form of leadership he also poses direct questions about Obama's sustained accountability to the Black community and the nation at large and his capacity to enact the change that was the cornerstone of his campaign: "I'm thinkin' I can trust this brother/but will he keep it real?/every innocent nigga in jail gets out on appeal/when he wins, will he really care still?"[13] This suggests that despite an abiding sense of optimism—the "hope" that was so central to the campaign—voters were not simply granting Obama a free pass.

Some hip-hop critics, such as independent artists Immortal Technique or political commentator Davey D, remain skeptical of Obama's capacity to enact real change, citing the restrictions of elected office and the tendency among so many Democratic leaders to cleave toward mainstream liberal interests in order to enact moderate change. Such skepticism serves as an important reminder that the black electorate is not a unified or homogeneous entity and that, even though there is tacit support for Obama's presidency, there remain serious concerns about the president's objectives and administrative strategies. Many hip-hop critics sought a more explicitly progressive and non-centrist political stance and overt resistance to the international abuses of justice and forces of global capitalist exploitation and neo-colonialism. The sentiment among many in the hip-hop community remains that Obama's words must translate into workable policies and his declarations of "change" must be accompanied by measurable outcomes that improve the options and well-being of low-class and struggling individuals and families not just in the United States but throughout the world wherever repression reigns.

Broad and lasting social change is not, of course, entirely Obama's to enact. His community organizing experience is founded on the capacity to encourage localities to define their needs and means of attaining resources as well as enabling political self-advocacy. As Troy Nkrumah of the National Hip-Hop Political Convention explains,

> *hip-hop culture has mobilized and organized young people to become more politically engaged [...]. There is no denying [Obama] has excited a lot of street cats that might not have engaged if it were not for his candidacy (Hale, 2008: 64).*

The numbers bear out Nkrumah's comment: During the 2008 Democratic campaign, "an overwhelming 78 percent of black voters chose Obama over (Hillary) Clinton and (John) Edwards" (Fraser, 2009: 27); in the presidential election, there was a notable increase of participation among Hispanic and African-American voters with each increasing over 2004 figures while the overall percentage of white non-Hispanic voters dipped slightly. Polls indicate that, "young people in general and blacks in particular were the most energized by Mr. Obama's candidacy" (Roberts, 2009: A[14]). Obama's victory mitigates, if only partially and momentarily, the widely cited paucity of black leadership in America. His background as a street-level community organizer underscores his connection to the 'hood, to the city, and to hip-hop culture more generally.

The Aftermath: What Changed?

As Obama's first year in office comes to a close, it is appropriate to ask what has changed. It is amply evident in hip-hop's underground and commercial arenas alike that the monumental historical transformation is taken quite seriously. Perhaps most notable are the ways in which young people in America have taken up Obama's sense of community responsibility and his subsequent call to service. Among the nation's 2009 graduating class there was an increase of university students professing a desire to work in service positions with low pay and no glamour (Rimer, 2009). There is also a rising trend of engagement as neighborhood volunteers and community associations spring to life, strengthening social bonds through civic responsibility (Gowen, 2009).

These trends correspond with hip-hop's distinct forms of community organizing and civic engagement. Today, every U.S. city of scale can claim a number of hip-hop oriented youth agencies (something that is also increasingly true on a global scale with youth advocacy initiatives and teen agencies emerging in cities such as London, Paris, Frankfurt, and Rio de Janeiro). Hip-hop oriented youth agencies and those who work for them are engaged in what I call "hood work," a term that enunciates and amplifies the locale of the urban 'hood that is also the locus of authenticity and value in hip-hop culture (Forman, 2002).

The primary mission among 'hood workers is to educate youth about their life options and about positive, pro-social attitudes and behaviors. These include: peaceful conflict resolution and an anti-gang stance; improved relations with law enforcement officers leading to the rejection of racial profiling practices and reduced incidents of police brutality; self-advocacy pertaining to school and education reform, criminal justice reform, and employment initiatives; teaching safer sex practices and teen pregnancy education; voter registration and political awareness; and a range of other public health issues that impact the lives of young urban citizens of all racial and ethnic backgrounds and their communities. 'Hood workers comprise an intervening force; the youth agencies directly engage urban youth, drawing them from negative and potentially deadly options including gang membership and street criminality and providing safe spaces where they can learn hip-hop skills and arts as well as developing political and community organizing abilities and community responsibilities that can positively impact themselves and others. These initiatives fall directly within the Obama model of civic responsibility and leadership.

Indeed, it is also common that 'hood work agencies offer a pointed critique of hip-hop itself, castigating certain popular artists and the major media corporations (such as Viacom, corporate owner of both MTV and BET) that portray degrading, stereotypical or negative images of black or Latino men and women (Lee, 2007). They acknowledge that the relentless circulation of images and discourses that promote negative and nihilistic values is part of a wider problem, influencing the perceptions if not necessarily the actions of literally millions of young hip-hop fans.[14] In an attempt to subvert these ubiquitous messages, 'hood workers assist youth in producing their own counter-hegemonic and resistant messages that challenge the dominant commercial discourses of gangsta rap or the accompanying violent, sexist/misogynistic, and materialist content of music, film, and video.

The terms "empowerment," "agency" and "responsibility" are commonly employed among 'hood workers and there is a pronounced emphasis toward "conscious hip-hop" and the employment of politically engaged and pro-social themes and images, merging the local crises confronted by youth with larger national and global issues. With the instantaneous global reach of the Internet, localized constituencies are able to mobilize transnational critiques of corporate media and of big government, global economic and military intervention, and cultural imperialism. Globally dispersed hip-hop artists and 'hood work agencies are also in better communication, learning from one another, exchanging aesthetic influences as well as exploring one another's "best practices" for greater effectiveness.

This all corresponds with Obama's own trajectory, enacting change at the local level while repairing strained global relations and employing political policies that might produce greater peace and sustained prosperity on an international scale. In this sense, just as the Obama presidency evolves and adjusts to ever-shifting conditions, so, too, does hip-hop evolve, transforming within the contexts of global/local dynamics and within a framework of indomitable spirit and hope.

Notes

1 Pubic Enemy's platinum albums (awarded for sales of at least one million units) include *It Takes a Nation of Millions to Hold Us Back*, 1988; *Fear of a Black Planet*, 1990; and *Apocalypse 91... The Enemy Strikes Black*, 1991. Public Enemy also reached gold album status (500.000 copies sold) with *Yo! Bum Rush the Show*, 1987 and *Muse Sick-n-Hour Mess Age*, 1994.

2 For a series of analytical essays about hip-hop and radical politics, see the special issue of *Socialism and Democracy: Hip Hop, Race, and Cultural Politics* 8:2 (2004).

3 The underground is a multivalent spatial concept, on the one hand referring to non-mainstream and non-commercial aspects of cultural production and, on the other hand, as a site of socio-political resistance to institutional power and authority.

Hip-hop has traditionally had a solid allegiance to underground practices among demographic groups that are most strongly affiliated with alternative or radical ideologies.

4 There are also several prominent hip-hop organizations in the U.S. dedicated to enacting progressive political change, including the Hip-Hop Summit Action Network and the National Hip-Hop Political Convention. With an advisory board comprised of twenty-three members of the U.S. Congress and Chaired by Congresswoman Barbara Lee, the stated mission of The Hip Hop Caucus is "to organize young people in urban communities to be active in elections, policymaking, and service projects, as a means to address and end urban poverty for future generations." There are also countless locally responsive grassroots hip-hop agencies across the nation.

5 Hip-hop tracks about Katrina proliferated after the tragedy. The Harvard Hip-Hop Archive offers a very partial list, including B. Down and Big Rags, "Katrina"; Jay Electronica, "When the Levees Broke"; Jay-Z, "Minority Report"; Lil Wayne, "Georgia Bush"; Lil Wayne with Robin Thicke, "Tie My Needs"; Papoose and Razah, "Mother Nature."

6 See Harvard University Hip-Hop Archive, http://www.hiphoparchive.org/prepare-yourself/katrina-knows (accessed April 10, 2010).

7 For a detailed account of the injection of race into the 2008 campaign and election, see Fraser, 2009.

8 See Jones, 2008.

9 In a pre-election interview with *Rolling Stone* magazine, Obama revealed an impressively wide range of musical influences (including hip-hop, rock, folk, and classical music), citing Stevie Wonder as his "musical hero" (Wenner, 2008).

10 At the 2008 Republican National Convention, Republican Vice-Presidential candidate Sarah Palin ridiculed Obama's service background, suggesting that he was *merely* engaged in localized community issues: "I guess a small-town mayor is sort of like a 'community organizer,' except that you have actual responsibilities." This attitude reveals an altogether common dismissal of local political activism and, further, a disdain for the social conditions and contexts of an impoverished urban milieu that requires committed advocates such as community organizers.

11 In a protracted legal case concerning the Obama image that is reminiscent of various rap music copyright cases over the years, the Associated Press sued Fairey for copyright infringement. In October 2009, Fairey admitted in court that he had lied about the source of the photo (taken by press photographer Mannie Garcia) but he defended his right to artistically manipulate the image under the fair use principle.

12 Shakur's "Changes" includes the lines, "and though it seems heaven sent, we ain't ready to have a black president."

13 Countless mainstream and underground artists released tracks referring to or explicitly endorsing Obama, many of which can be accessed on YouTube. For one of the first scholarly analyses of an Obama track—"My President" by the Atlanta MC Young Jeezy—see Nielson, 2009.

14 The President expresses his awareness and concern about hip-hop's less savory content, noting, "I am troubled sometimes by the misogyny and materialism of a lot of rap lyrics, but I think the genius of the art form has shifted the culture and helped to desegregate music [...]. It would be nice if I could have my daughters listen to their music without me worrying that they were getting bad images of themselves" (Wenner, 2008).

8

Beyoncé and the Politicization of Popular Culture

Juliet Winter

Juliet Winter is a PhD candidate and associate lecturer at the University of Winchester in England. Her research focuses on constructs of racial and gendered identity in the contemporary US, particularly focusing on representations of race and gender in American popular culture, politics, and sports.

Through looking at the evolution of Beyoncé's depiction of feminism in her music, which Winter argues reached its zenith with her 2016 album Lemonade, *we can see that there is space for popular culture to move from nonpolitical, relatively vapid and oversimplified notions of feminism and into a complex political discussion. While Beyoncé is known for being at the top of the popular culture world, her later work indicates that she does not allow her popularity as an artist and celebrity to keep her from exploring issues of race, gender, and oppression in her work. Through addressing these issues in her music, Winter argues that Beyoncé has succeeded at starting important political conversations.*

M uch of Beyoncé's career has been defined by an image that has spoken largely to notions of the form of "girl power"

"Beyoncé's 'Lemonade': A Complex and Intersectional Exploration of Racial and Gendered Identity," by Juliet Winter, U.S. Studies Online, June 6, 2016, http://www.baas.ac.uk/usso/beyonces-lemonade-a-complex-and-intersectional-exploration-of-racial-and-gendered-identity/. Licensed under CC BY 3.0.

and independence that we associate with the emergence of postfeminist popular culture in the 1990s. Largely conceptualised as a "non-political" feminist discourse, manifestations of postfeminism in popular culture have been characterised by notions of choice, individualism and the re-commodification of femininity. Examples may include artists such as Britney Spears, Christina Aguilera and Katy Perry, whose works speak to the complexity of female independence and hyper-femininity. These characteristics are particularly evident in Beyoncé's work within Destiny's Child (notably with tracks such as "Independent Woman" and "Survivor") as well as her early solo career (which included the singles "If I Were a Boy" and "Single Ladies"). However, her growing domination of—and influence within—the popular music industry has placed Beyoncé in a seemingly unique position in popular cultural spheres, and in turn has opened the door for her engagement with more politically fuelled themes in her music. Direct references to political feminism in her 2013 visual album, *Beyoncé*, signified a very intentional and tangible shift in her negotiation of gender and self-image.

The release of *Lemonade* (2016)[1] and its featured tracks take this further by moving beyond the often problematically white nature of postfeminism—with critics Diana Negra and Yvonne Tasker arguing that postfeminism is "white and middle class by default"[2]—and into the much more current conceptualisations of intersectional "fourth wave" feminist discourse. Delving deeper into *Lemonade* as an important cultural text is vital therefore if we are to understand further its political and personal constructs of race and gender, and why Beyoncé has chosen this moment to so explicitly represent her own blackness and feminist stance.

Lemonade goes beyond the semi-surface level engagement with feminist discourse in *Beyoncé* and delves into a much more complex and intersectional exploration of constructed racial and gendered identity and oppression. It also goes far deeper than the much debated infidelity narrative of the text, which has so far garnered much attention and speculation on social media.

Beyond this, *Lemonade* uses distinct visual and lyrical references to transcend the strict social boundaries established by historic systems of patriarchy and racial hierarchy in the United States. It notably deconstructs and contradicts the binaries of "blackness" and "whiteness," and in doing so has created a space that is not only inclusive of women of colour, but places them at the front and centre of the narrative.

Furthermore, *Lemonade* speaks to the challenge of defining black identity, history and heritage, while simultaneously celebrating blackness, womanhood and humanism. Beyoncé's negotiation of her own racial and gendered identity—in the track "Formation" in particular—celebrates personal and collective black heritage whilst at the same time calling for America to rethink its strict notions of "blackness" and "whiteness." References to the visual iconography of the South—notably the use of plantation houses, Live Oaks, swamplands, antebellum costume and a focus on New Orleans—alongside lyrical references to her "bama" roots, construct Beyoncé's own blackness as that which sits within a collective African American history and heritage. In consciously positioning herself within the space of "authentic" blackness (despite her commercial and economic success within the whiteness of postfeminist popular culture and the "industry" more widely), Beyoncé is able to unapologetically celebrate black identity and womanhood, and very publically expose issues of discrimination in the United States.

The tracks "Forward" and "Freedom" react directly to racial injustice, with reference to the Black Lives Matter movement used to represent failed promises of freedom while also suggesting the need for strength, resistance and black self-determination. It is here that the overarching infidelity narrative seems to serve more so as a metaphor, drawing on the parallels of failed promise, contradiction and subordination that have come to shape the collective experience of African Americans—and African American women in particular—through histories and legacies of slavery, segregation and discrimination in the United States.

These themes are present—both overtly and subtly—throughout the text, and tend to focus on black women with the exception of the track "Daddy Lessons," which seemingly shifts the focus to black men's struggles with ideological and often unattainable notions of patriarchal masculinity. Calls for women to "get in formation" speak to the collective political activism of second wave and black feminist movements of the 1960s, '70s and '80s, and place black women as both a means to and measure of change. There is a particular emphasis throughout the text on the need for self-determined black female excellence, with lyrics such as, "I'ma keep running, cause a winner don't quit on themselves" in "Freedom" and, "I dream it, I work hard, I grind 'til I own it" in "Formation." Furthermore, the appearance of a number of famous black women who have succeeded within the whiteness of mainstream sport and popular culture—notably tennis star Serena Williams, the featured image and music of Nina Simone, and up and coming stars Chloe and Halle Bailey, Amandla Stenberg, Zendaya, and Lisa-Kainde and Naomi Diaz— all speak to notions of black female excellence.

Throughout *Lemonade* Beyoncé focuses on past, present and future, using poetry from Somalie-British poet Warsan Shire, and visual iconography to tell a story of a collective black female identity as that which has long been shaped by others. She speaks to Melissa Harris-Perry's concept of the "crooked room"[3] throughout the text, bringing into the mainstream the experience of black women and their inability to "stand upright" in an America long shaped by systems of white patriarchy. Clips of black women bound together by white garments suggestive of straightjackets, and the use of narrative poetry that speaks to the challenge of negotiating "white" standards of femininity—"I can wear her skin over mine; her hair over mine; her hands as gloves…"[4]—seek to highlight the "double bind" of racist and sexist oppression experienced by women of colour throughout America's history.

In exploring constructed racial and gendered identity as a product of privileged systems of whiteness Beyoncé highlights the still very present social and political structures that shape the lives of people of colour, women and minorities around the world today. In attempting to explore and deconstruct definitions of race and gender she creates a wide-reaching dialogue that captures the zeitgeist of the current social and political moment in the United States. While not without its faults—some critics question how she constructs her own blackness within the text—Beyoncé has successfully engaged audiences in these conversations, and in doing so has simultaneously brought women of colour into the predominantly white sphere of American popular culture and music. As such, *Lemonade* becomes a significant and important cultural text that reacts to current political and social issues facing African American communities and women of colour in the twenty-first century. While Beyoncé remains in a uniquely influential position within the music industry and continues to negotiate issues of race, gender and feminism through her music and public persona, she will continue to engage audiences in conversations surrounding identity, inequality and representation, and in doing so becomes an important figure that cultural critics and feminist scholars must engage with.

Notes

[1] Beyoncé, *Lemonade*, Parkwood Entertainment, Columbia. 2016. CD.

[2] Yvonne Tasker and Diane Negra, *Interrogating Postfeminism: Gender and the Politics of Popular Culture*, Duke University Press, 2007. Pp2.

[3] Harris-Perry, Melissa V. *Sister Citizen: Shame, Stereotypes, and Black Women in America*, Yale University Press; London. 2011.

[4] Poetry from Warsan Shire, credited with Film Adaptation and Poetry in *Lemonade*; Parkwood Entertainment, 2016.

9

Well-Meaning Celebrities Can Cause Harm with Humanitarian Campaigns

Andres Jimenez

Andres Jimenez lives, writes, and works in San Jose, Costa Rica. He is an international conflict analyst and a trainer in nonviolent methods of conflict resolution.

Can individuals from a Washington think tank, foreign NGO, or Ivy League university truly understand humanitarian crises and conflicts half a world away? Some argue not. But this issue becomes exacerbated when celebrities determine that there are problems that need to be fixed in faraway places, and that they have been appointed to address them. Opponents of this type of intervention contend that these problems are much too complicated for remote experts to understand and that the well-intentioned campaigns led by celebrities are doing more harm than good in the long run.

As I sat in the stands of Pece Stadium in the northern Uganda town of Gulu on a sunny Sunday morning, a couple of young men made their way close to where I was sitting. We struck up a conversation, and they said that it was a pity that I had not witnessed the event that had taken place not long before my arrival in town a few weeks earlier.

My new friends began to describe how there had been a massive gathering in the stadium for the screening of a video put together by a foreign NGO. The video had profoundly upset a significant amount of those present that evening, and a riot broke out. I realized that, of course, they were talking about the launch of the first Kony 2012 video campaign by the U.S.-based organization Invisible Children. The video's portrayal of the over two-decade-long conflict had deeply angered many of those who had endured it firsthand. The crowd ended up having to be dispersed by police and tear gas.

As I listened to the men's account of how the crowd's anger turned to violence, I could hardly keep myself from thinking how emblematic and representative such an event was of countless celebrity-fueled, do-good awareness campaigns that I had already had the misfortune to witness over the years.

The tragedy behind these sorts of campaigns is that they are motivated by the belief that problems around the world remain unresolved due to the lack of international awareness of their existence or global commitment to resolve them. If only enough people knew and cared about a certain conflict or problem, the assumption goes, then the combined energy and support could be harnessed in order to trigger an immediate flood of solutions. Any action taken toward this end is therefore righteous and will to put us a step closer to fixing the problem; surely any little bit of help must be better than nothing.

It is this mindset that has motivated celebrities like the rock star Bono to take up the causes of debt cancelation, the increase in foreign aid and the promotion of the Millennium Development Goals. Actor George Clooney has taken great interest in Darfur; Madonna and Oprah Winfrey have embraced the fight for girls' education in Africa, while Angelina Jolie knocks at the doors of the major centers of power as a UNHCR Goodwill Ambassador to promote support for humanitarian relief. Unfortunately, many of the policies and remedies promoted by this ever-growing influx of celebrity activists have been heavily criticized for being paternalistic, detached from reality and often dangerously counterproductive.

However, far from being deterred, celebrity activists find solace in the assurances of so-called experts, specialists and analysts who fill the ranks of leading international organizations, Washington think tanks and Ivy League universities. These people are the Nicholas Kristofs and the Jeffry Sachses of the world who often find their self-assurance and sense of certainty in their Ivy League educations, in the power that their positions grant them or in the titles that they hold. Their almost complete confidence in their predictions and analyses, combined with the allure of celebrity, emboldens them to leap at the opportunity to promote what they consider to be the solutions for conflicts whose complexities they only superficially grasp.

Celebrity-led campaigns do often prove to be highly successful in generating broad public support. This is because they draw on the self-serving guilt trips that lead many people to believe that their privileged position has invested them with the burden and the responsibility to save those less fortunate from their plight. Celebrity activists provide us with a powerful outlet for our guilty consciences and our self-serving views of history. What better way to liberate ourselves from this burden than by taking up a global cause in a far-away land, and who better to show us the way to do it than our favorite celebrities?

My experience working with armed conflicts and humanitarian crises has shown me the disastrous effects that such views tend to have on the ground. Away from the fantasy world of easy-to-understand, black-and-white, single-story views of a conflict lays a world of complexity, depth and uncertainty. With the embrace of complexity we are able to discover that the way we seek to approach and work within a conflict must be incredibly flexible and diverse.

We need to distance ourselves from the powerful desire to follow simple solutions drafted by experts in conference rooms half a world away. We should begin, above all, by focusing on the creative energy already present among the local actors in a conflict in order to discover context-specific strategies that can help us to transform it.

Sadly, this approach does not fit well in a five-minute YouTube video or an inspirational TED Talk. Our fascination with pre-packaged solutions and our short attention spans are incompatible with appreciation for true complexity, humility and unpredictability.

If you feel invested in a cause, engage it with all your passion, but tread carefully. Ask yourself why you even care about this conflict in the first place. Whose voices are you listening to about it? Whose interests are they serving? What is already being tried by local actors on the ground? And, most importantly, why should you become involved?

If you do decide to take that leap, then start by listening rather than preaching, facilitating rather than commanding, cooperating rather than defeating, creating organically rather than planning mechanically, and seeking to unsettle the status quo rather than trying to control it in its entirety. Being told that you have an urgent responsibility to act in order to help solve a conflict that you hardly even knew existed in the first place is the first step down a slippery slope of continuous despair, wasted goodwill and neo-colonialism.

10

Can Celebrities Help Save the Environment?

Elizabeth Duthie, Diogo Veríssimo, Aidan Keane,
and Andrew T. Knight

Elizabeth Duthie is affiliated with the department of life sciences at Imperial College London's Silwood Park campus. Diogo Veríssimo is affiliated with the Andrew Young School of Policy Studies at Georgia State University. Aidan Keane is affiliated with the School of Geosciences at the University of Edinburgh. Aidan T. Knight is also affiliated with the Imperial College London's department of life sciences, as well as the Centre of Excellence in Environmental Decisions at the University of Queensland, the department of botany at Nelson Mandela Metropolitan University, and the Silwood Group.

The research discussed in this viewpoint explores the effect celebrity campaigns have on natural conservation NGOs, examining the efficacy of such campaigns and the factors that may help determine whether the campaign will succeed. The study examines the ways test subjects respond to campaigns featuring different kinds of celebrities, including Prince William (Duke of Cambridge and second in line for the British throne), David Beckham (soccer star), Chris Packham (a naturalist and television personality), and Crawford Allan (a wildlife expert and Senior Director of the World Wildlife Fund).

"The Effectiveness of Celebrities in Conservation Marketing," by Elizabeth Duthie, Diogo Veríssimo, Aidan Keane and Andrew T. Knight, National Center for Biotechnology Information, July 7, 2017, https://www.ncbi.nlm.nih.gov/pmc/articles/PMC5501471/. Licensed under CC BY 4.0.

It is increasingly acknowledged that effective conservation is ultimately dependent on influencing human attitudes and behavior. As with most businesses, conservation non-governmental organizations (NGOs) are dependent on marketing their products and services to the broader populous to effectively and efficiently realize their goals. The field of conservation marketing is increasingly being recognised as an important component in the conservation communities' toolkit, demonstrated recently by the formation of the Society for Conservation Biology's Conservation Marketing and Engagement Working Group (ConsMark). A key strategy in marketing conservation has been the use of celebrities to promote environmental and conservation NGOs and their work. For example, His Royal Highness The Duke of Cambridge was instrumental in the creation of the *United For Wildlife* partnership, whilst American actors Harrison Ford and Leonardo DiCaprio are, respectively, the Vice-Chair for Conservation Internationals' Board of Directors and donor, campaigner and board member of the World Wildlife Fund (WWF-US). Leonardo DiCaprio's acceptance speech at the 2016 Academy Awards focused on climate change, resulting in a substantially higher volume of news articles, social media posts and information searches than either the 2015 Conference of the Parties or Earth Day.

The marketing industry has developed a range of theories and selection techniques over the last six decades to identify the most effective celebrity attributes for specific types of campaigns. These include the source credibility model, which posits that celebrities considered knowledgeable and trustworthy positively impact on the effectiveness of a marketing campaign, and the product match-up hypothesis, which posits the effectiveness of an advertising campaign increases when there is a clear and identifiable link between the celebrity and a product or service. However, despite the wide use of celebrities for marketing products, the empirical literature is equivocal on the effectiveness of celebrity endorsement. Pringle argues that celebrities act as indicators of quality, providing a brand with increased publicity and exposure as well as access to a celebrity's audience. In addition, a brand is linked by association to desirable qualities that consumers believe a celebrity to possess. Consequently celebrity endorsement may generate and retain attention, increase product recall rates in overly cluttered markets, and can be a powerful predictor of an intention-to-purchase products or services. However, some studies have found no significant positive effect of celebrity endorsement and that celebrity endorsement does not guarantee mass media coverage. If not carefully managed, celebrities, as with flagship species used to promote conservation campaigns, may become over-exposed by being associated with too many campaigns, thus diluting their effectiveness. It may even more fundamentally be that celebrity endorsement targeting the broader public is misplaced, as most donations arise from personal relationships, as opposed to celebrity influence.

[...]

Results

Use and Evaluation of Celebrities by Organizations

Of the U.K. conservation organizations, all used celebrities to a greater or lesser extent in their marketing and/or fund-raising work and all considered celebrities valuable. Celebrity use differed across organizations, some seeking "credibility" by association, whilst others sought increased social media and press engagement. Accessing new market sectors often involved celebrities appearing at fund-raising events (e.g., as after dinner speakers) to attract high net-worth individuals in influential careers ("elites") with whom the organization planned to build a relationship.

All organizations monitored their celebrity-based marketing using web analytics, column inches or social media engagement. Only one of the 10 conservation organizations, and both humanitarian organizations, applied formal evaluation procedures.

No evaluation of the effectiveness of specific celebrity attributes was conducted by any organization.

All conservation organizations lacked a strategy for developing and maintaining celebrity partnerships. Most had no formal celebrity engagement strategy, and interactions with celebrities were usually opportunistic and often conducted in an *ad hoc* manner.

Every organization stated they had not paid a celebrity to appear or act as a spokesperson, particularly if the celebrity was a patron or trustee. Some organizations would cover celebrities' costs incurred by involvement (e.g., travel costs).

The Effectiveness of Celebrity Endorsement

Do celebrities ensure higher WTE [willingness to engage]? Respondents displayed higher WTE with a celebrity compared to the control. The effect of celebrity was linked to the respondents' beliefs about the celebrities featured in the advertisements. Respondents who believed that other people would be influenced by the support of the celebrity displayed substantially higher WTE than those who did not. Respondents reporting a celebrity's statement caught their attention or that they often engage with promotional images displayed higher WTE. Smaller positive effects occurred where respondents displayed interest in why a celebrity supported a campaign or if they believed the celebrity was knowledgeable about it.

Respondents' beliefs about why a celebrity was appearing in an advertisement influenced willingness-to-engage. Those who believed a celebrity appeared because a friend had asked or because they were being paid were more likely to engage. Conversely, those believing a celebrity appeared to improve their own profile were less likely to.

Older respondents, those who supported one or more conservation NGOs and those who donated to charities focused on international issues, were also more willing-to-engage. In combination, scenario-based predictions from our fitted models suggest an individual's characteristics can substantially affect their WTE. For example, the fitted model predicts that 43.6% of females, aged 55–64, with a university degree and living in the countryside would engage with Prince William, Duke of Cambridge, compared with only 15.3% of males, aged 16–24, with no university degree and living in a major city (in both cases considering scenarios where the individuals are employed, do not support any conservation NGOs and do not donate to any charities).

Do celebrities increase message recall? Respondents were less likely to recall an advertisement message if it featured a celebrity than if it featured the control. Aside from the specific celebrity featured in the advertisements, few other variables predicted recall well. Recall was somewhat lower amongst older and female respondents but higher amongst those who reported donating to religious charities (but no other predictors produced clear effects.

Why do respondents choose one celebrity over another? When presented with all four advertisements and asked to choose which they preferred, the advertisement featuring Chris Packham was the most popular (chosen by 36.9% of respondents), followed by Prince William, Duke of Cambridge (34.2%), David Beckham (16.8%) and Crawford Allan (12.1%).

Respondents' choice was predicted by advertisement characteristics, stated preference for a specific celebrity, and demographic characteristics. The most important advertisement characteristics were the photograph, then the statement. Respondents were more likely to choose a celebrity when they reported that "His photograph caught my eye" or "His statement made me want to find out more."

Respondents were also more likely to choose a celebrity if they believed he cared about, was knowledgeable about, or was known to support a specified issue. Celebrities thought to be using an issue to improve or raise his own profile or might be being paid for their involvement were less likely to be preferred.

Respondents who explained their choice by stating "I like him more than the others" were much more likely to prefer Prince William, Duke of Cambridge, followed by David Beckham, Chris Packham and Crawford Allan. Respondents who explained their choice by stating "His photo caught my eye" were more likely to choose David Beckham, while those who stated "I already knew about his support for this" most often chose Prince William, Duke of Cambridge or Chris Packham. Conversely, those who selected "I believe he is the most knowledgeable about this issue" were most likely to choose Crawford Allan, followed by Chris Packham and were very unlikely to choose Prince William, Duke of Cambridge or David Beckham.

Discussion

Marketing, having existed in some form since humans started trading, has a well-established body of theory, and is a key activity in business practice. It has evolved from concentrating on the product to the current focus on relationship marketing; the constant connection and interplay between the consumer, product and brand. Consequently many NGOs are increasingly using new marketing thinking and practice to guide their strategies and communications. Marketing strategies provide the reference point for all decisions an organization makes about its marketing concepts and outputs and are critically important for ensuring resources are used effectively and brand reputation is maintained and developed. The conservation NGOs in this study, and possibly those more generally, lack a dedicated celebrity endorsement strategy. This is problematic, given the on-going and extensive reliance upon celebrity endorsement and its perceived effectiveness. Furthermore, a lack of formal celebrity endorsement strategy results in a failure to evaluate celebrity campaigns and therefore understand the ways in which to maximize the return-on-investment (ROI). This study found that whilst celebrities can be beneficial in eliciting positive WTE behavior, they can have a negative effect on message recall, and the choice of celebrity can play a critical role in the effectiveness of a campaign.

The role of evaluation and evidence-based analysis is considered a priority within the marketing industry, just as it is within the conservation community. However, while conservation organizations commonly use celebrities to market their campaigns, our results suggest that they rarely pre-test or evaluate (i.e., employ evidence for) their effectiveness. Our findings suggest that celebrity endorsement is indeed able to generate higher levels of WTE amongst the public, corroborating the results of previous studies. However, they also challenge the idea that celebrity endorsement is always beneficial, regardless of application—a view that was commonly expressed in our interviews with representatives of conservation organizations—by showing that the public's WTE with celebrities in conservation campaigns is nuanced, and driven by multiple factors, with no one approach or technique being universally effective.

Celebrities therefore may not always be the most effective choice for a marketing campaign and appropriate evaluation is essential. For example, in accordance with the principles of the Source Credibility Model, we found that celebrities who were considered to be knowledgeable about an issue generated significantly higher levels of WTE. As Till & Busler argue, this suggests that celebrity endorsers should ideally be seen to possess expertise about the product or topic they are promoting. Interestingly, whilst Chris Packham was viewed as being highly knowledgeable about the illegal wildlife trade, he had never officially spoken about the issue prior to the data collection period. Thus, his perceived expertise most likely derives from his role as a nature documentary presenter and campaigner on various wildlife and conservation related issues. By contrast, Crawford Allan was viewed as the most knowledgeable (understandably, given his role as Senior Director for Wildlife Crime at Traffic), but this expertise alone was not enough to generate higher levels of engagement.

It is also important that evaluations of the effectiveness of celebrity endorsement take great care when selecting their measures of success. Crucially, while we found that celebrity endorsement generates higher WTE, it also led to lower recall of the issues being communicated. There are several factors that may have contributed to this finding. One possibility is that if a celebrity's support for a broader issue is well established, that existing association might complicate attempts to communicate a more specific message, resulting in an ineffective campaign. For example, Prince William, Duke of Cambridge has become well known for his involvement in wildlife conservation (despite the British Royal Family's ongoing interest and participation in blood sports) and particularly his role in forming *United for Wildlife*, a collection of seven conservation organizations combatting the illegal trade in wildlife. Given the extensive press exposure *United for Wildlife* has received, particularly in the United Kingdom, under the product match-up hypothesis it would have been reasonable to expect that he would elicit higher levels of recall from respondents in the survey. In fact, while levels of full recall were low, he generated reasonable levels of incomplete recall, suggesting that respondents may only have been able to recall that Prince William was associated with wildlife conservation in general. They were not able to remember the exact nature of the issue he was endorsing. A second possibility relates to the directed nature of the survey, in which respondents were asked to look at the advertisement and answer questions accordingly. This is not reflective of the contextual nature of marketing, with respondents instructed to examine an advertisement they might otherwise ignore. Additionally, given the unfamiliarity of Crawford Allan for the majority of respondents, additional cognitive processing would have been necessary, thus resulting in higher levels of recall.

While promoting more widespread evaluation of celebrity endorsement—and conservation marketing more generally—we recognize that conservation organizations face multiple barriers that might hinder its adoption. In addition to pressure on resources (financial, staff time and arguably staff capacity) within conservation NGOs, it is understandable that organizations do not want to risk wasting a celebrity endorsement opportunity. The majority of celebrity endorsement in conservation marketing is reliant on goodwill and personal connections. With little formal guidance available for selecting an endorser, let alone a specific marketing technique for use, conservation organizations are left grasping at any celebrity endorsement opportunity available. As shown by this study, this does not necessarily translate into effective marketing, and in some cases could potentially be detrimental to an issue or organization. Furthermore, conservation organizations are rarely approached by celebrities seeking partnership opportunities. Instead, organizations draw-up a "wish list" of celebrities they hope to engage with, and successively work down the list until they find ones who are willing and available. Whilst it is understandable that for many organizations this is the only process available to them to secure celebrity endorsement, it runs a substantial risk of identifying a celebrity who exerts little, or worse, negative influence, particularly given the body of literature reinforcing the importance of celebrity endorser and brand congruence.

It is vital to ensure campaigns are as effective as possible, which is determined by factors including the public perception of the brand and the celebrity endorsement itself. Greater research is required to ensure celebrity endorsement is used in the most effective way, for example to avoid the perception that their involvement is undermining or belittling the issue. Future work should aim to understand the celebrity attributes that are most effective, and the demographic groups they are most effective on. Understanding the role celebrities play in communicating conservation ideas and issues at both global and local levels is critical for ensuring celebrity endorsers are used strategically and appropriately. Understanding the effect celebrity endorsement has on decision- and policy-makers will allow the conservation community to maximize the return-on-investment of their marketing campaigns. It is also important to understand if, and in what contexts, charismatic species of fauna and flora, or other elements of nature, are more effective than human celebrities in communicating conservation messages to the public, positively changing behavior and raising funds.

Conclusion

Celebrity endorsement is used to market conservation projects and programmes, however the reasons conservation NGOs adopt this technique is rarely explored. Furthermore their effectiveness is rarely investigated.

Celebrity endorsement is not unequivocally effective, and there is increasing philanthropic fatigue from the public. Therefore a key recommendation, based on the marketing literature, and the findings from this study, are for conservation organizations to focus on building brand awareness and equity. Not only will increased brand presence in the market increase public engagement, but increased brand equity (the assets such as name recognition and perceived quality that are connected to a brand and give a product or service its value) will serve as a useful tool in securing celebrity endorsement. Given the lack of marketing research currently conducted by conservation organizations, this is an area where the research community could make a substantial and useful contribution to conservation organizations. Researchers can bypass the risk to reputation and celebrity endorser relationships that conservation organizations may carry if they undertake the research themselves. Whilst celebrities can prove more effective in generating positive WTE behaviour, they might not be as effective at generating full campaign message recall and factors such as credibility, likeability and a connection between the campaign and endorser are critical. This study shows the role testing and evaluation can play in ensuring the maximum impact of celebrity endorsers and how they can be harnessed to not only raise funds for conservation, but also to raise awareness and effect behaviour change.

11

The Presidency and the Collision of Politics and Entertainment

Andrew Trounson

Andrew Trounson is the senior editor for Pursuit, *the University of Melbourne's content website.*

While certain factors were against the Democrats in the 2016 presidential election—indeed, it is almost unprecedented for a political party to win three presidential elections in a row—there is still the chance that celebrity politicians may be an enduring trend. Political journalist and expert Matt Bai claims that President Trump's experience as an entertainer enabled him to stand out among the field of Republican candidates and allowed him to better determine what voters wanted from him. Because of their crowd-pleasing expertise, celebrities could continue to succeed on the political stage.

D onald Trump is only the beginning.
America has already seen celebrities such as pro wrestler Jesse Ventura and body building actor Arnold Schwarzenegger make it as state governors. Are celebrity politicians the new normal?

Award-winning US journalist and author Matt Bai, who is National Political Columnist for Yahoo News and had a cameo role in hit political TV drama *House of Cards*, said Mr Trump had capitalised on a media glued to entertainment and ratings. And other ambitious celebrities are watching.

"We are entering a period where traditional paths of politics won't matter, and we as a media have to evaluate what it is we need to be covering about people, and what kind of scrutiny we need to bring to the process," Mr Bai told a seminar at the University of Melbourne's Centre for Advancing Journalism.

"If Trump loses and goes away, he isn't the end of something, he is the beginning of something," he said. "I don't know who they are, but I assure you that there are actors, tech-billionaires and athletes watching this from home and thinking 'I can do that, I can do it better, I can be more credible and I actually have something I want to do with the country.'"

Mr Bai said Mr Trump's candidacy had been made possible by a "collision of politics and entertainment," in which contemporary culture had become focused on the narrative stories of politicians rather than the substance of policy.

"Trump is the perfect embodiment of the entertainment culture in our politics and we as the media make that possible," Mr Bai told the audience.

In what was a crowded Republican Party primary contest, where there were initially 17 candidates, Mr Bai said the media focused on Mr Trump because of his entertainment value.

That starved the other candidates of oxygen and aided Mr Trump's campaign. That was despite, Mr Bai argued, Mr Trump having no ideology other than the promotion of his own brand. In effect, he said Mr Trump had simply "borrowed" the Republican Party.

"Trump is a pure entertainer, that is his ideology," Mr Bai said. "He wants to exploit the emotion in a room and he wants to hear the applause, and be talked about and validated. That, I believe, is the only thing that drives him."

Mr Bai said Mr Trump had exploited a general fear in America over the pace of change and the loss of jobs as economies globalised and automated. This fear had been further fanned by the 2001 terrorist attacks and the 2008 financial crisis. He said politicians had so far failed to squarely address this fear, alienating a large section of the electorate that Mr Trump had targeted.

Blame Game

"He heard this intense fear and found a place to put the blame— found a place to put the blame on immigrants, found a place to put the blame on political correctness, on liberal culture.

"There is a sort of smug rush to thought policing that has been going on in liberal quarters of America now for quite a while ... that people have lived with for long enough and Trump is giving them an outlet to voice their rage about that.

"People are scared and trying to work their way through a wrenching transformation and when you don't give them a vision for where we need to go and how we get there, then you invite someone like a Donald Trump to fill that vacuum ... but I don't think he has the answer.

"I think he is unleashing, exploiting and intensifying a very dangerous series of emotions without really offering anything by way of a persuasive solution."

Mr Bai said Mr Trump had also benefited from a broken primary election system in which fewer and fewer people were members of parties and actually voting. As a result the voice of the broader centre wasn't being heard.

He noted the *New York Times* had estimated that Mr Trump and Democrat challenger Hilary Clinton only secured 9 percent of the combined national vote in winning their respective nominations. "The primary system as it is currently constituted has outlived its usefulness."

Can Mr Trump go all the way and win the presidency? Mr Bai said history was against a Democratic win, noting that only once since 1951, when the Constitution was changed to limit any President to two terms, had a party won three consecutive terms in the White House—that was George Bush Snr in 1988. But he said Mr Trump's failure so far to become a more inclusive candidate meant it would be difficult for him to win.

"There are historical currents working against Clinton—she is a very distrusted nominee, and a very middling retail politician who has articulated a very muddled set of convictions for the presidency quite honestly," Mr Bai said. "But I think Trump had to make a turn, he had to be a better, more legitimate, more inclusive candidate and he hasn't. That frankly surprised me and I came to the conclusion that he lacked the capacity to do that.

"We have at least two and probably three debates to go through which can be very important, especially given how entertaining he can be for people, but I think that window (for Trump) is closing."

12

Does the Media Play a Significant Role in Elections?

Jonathan Stray

With master's degrees in both computer science and journalism, Jonathan Stray assists investigative journalists in making sense of large document sets as part of the Overview Project for the Associated Press. He also teaches computation journalism at Columbia University.

It seems intuitive that media plays a role in election results, but is this actually the case? If so, how much of an impact does it have? Computer analysis on large amounts of polling data has uncovered an interesting situation: media appears to play a role, but not a simple causal one, and it doesn't seem to affect all candidates equally. Coverage of political candidates is a complicated process, especially when it comes to how to cover these potential elected officials equally.

Whether your favorite candidate is popular or unpopular, it's always popular to blame the media. We see a lot of this right now in discussions of why Trump is in the lead or why Sanders isn't.

Usually the complaints have to do with what the media is saying about a candidate. But another theory says that it's the

"How much influence does the media really have over elections? Digging into the data," by Jonathan Stray, Nieman Foundation for Journalism at Harvard University, January 11, 2016. Reprinted by permission.

attention that matters. Good news or bad—maybe the important thing is just to be talked about.

Or maybe professional journalists have very little influence at all. Many people now get their news by clicking on articles from social media, where your friends and a filtering algorithm decide what you see.

So does the media still matter? Does attention get results for candidates, regardless of what is said? And if it does, how should journalists cover elections fairly and responsibly? These are the questions I wanted to try to answer, at least as they relate to the current U.S. presidential primaries.

Attention vs. Popularity

These are big questions about how the American political system works, far too big for simple answers. But you have to start somewhere, so I decided to compare the number of times each 2016 candidate has been mentioned in the U.S. mainstream media with their standing in national primary polls. To my surprise, the two line up almost exactly.

There's an uncanny agreement between the media attention and each candidate's standing in national primary polls. It's a textbook correlation.

Depending on what corner of the political universe you come from, it may surprise you to learn that both Trump and Sanders were covered in proportion to their poll results—at least online. Pretty much everyone was. The exceptions are Jeb Bush, who seems to have been covered twice as much as his standing would suggest, and Carson, who might have been slightly under-covered.

By simply counting the number of mentions, we're completely ignoring what journalists are actually saying, including whether the coverage was positive or negative. This data doesn't say anything at all about tone or frame or even what issues were discussed. All of these things might be very important in the larger context of democracy, but they seem to be less important in terms of primary poll results. While the story surely matters, it doesn't seem to matter as much as the attention. In particular, Trump has received much more negative coverage than his GOP competitors, to little apparent effect.

I admit I was a bit shocked to discover how closely the percentage of media mentions and the percentage of voter support align. But I'm also not the first to notice. Nate Silver found that this pattern holds in U.S. primary elections going back to 1980, though his model also incorporated favorability ratings. This correlation has also been noticed by previous political science researchers, though I haven't been able to find anywhere it's been seriously investigated.

So what's going on here? How do all the numbers just line up? Does this mean the media exert near-total control over the political process? Fortunately, no. To begin with, national primary polls don't predict the eventual nominee very well; state polls matter much more, because the nominating process happens one state at a time. But it seems reasonable to imagine that media attention has *some* effect on the polls. Yet journalists also *respond* to the polls, which means it isn't clear what's causing what.

Which Came First: The Media or the Polls?

If you're worried about the media's influence you're thinking of a causal relationship like this: media attention causes poll results.

But there are two other ways that these variables can become highly correlated. First, causality could go the other way. The polls could drive the media.

This isn't completely insane. Journalists have to follow audience attention or risk getting ignored. And if voters are also readers, a candidate who is twice as popular might get twice the number of views and shares. That matters when you're deciding what to cover—though it's hardly the only consideration. More on that later.

There's one more way to get a close relationship between media and polls: something else could be driving both of them. For example, attention on social media could drive both. A single post can go viral and reach millions without any involvement from professional journalists. Or perhaps endorsements from famous people and organizations are the key to influence, as political scientists have long suspected. And then there are the candidates themselves: anything they do might make them more (or less!) favorable with both the media and the public. In short we need to consider *every other thing*, and many of these things will drive media attention and voter preference in the same direction, causing a correlation like the one we've seen.

These are the basic causal forces, the only possible ways that media attention and polling results can become so closely aligned. We're going to need more information to figure out what is causing what.

One way to test for causality is to ask whether a change in coverage precedes a change in the polls, or vice versa. Here's the number of articles mentioning the right-wing U.K. Independence Party (UKIP) versus poll results, tracked over 11 years in the British press.

In the research of James Murphy of Southhampton University, we're looking at changes across time, rather than between parties. Yet once again, coverage and popularity follow each other closely. To determine which came first, Murphy built a statistical model that tries to predict this month's polls from the previous month's coverage, and vice versa. Whichever direction works better, that's the way the cause runs. But the results were inconclusive—they depended on exactly how the model was put together. This suggests that the causality goes both ways.

Trump's polls and mentions rose at about the same rate after he announced his candidacy, so at first glance it looks like the two are tied together. But media spikes don't always translate into polling spikes: Both debates produced a spike in coverage, but the polls actually decreased in the short term. The burst of coverage after he announced his plan to exclude Muslims does seem to line up with a bump in popularity, though.

John Sides of George Washington University has done a statistical analysis to try to tease out the causality in Trump's data and, once again, the results don't clearly favor the chicken or the egg. Instead, it seems that the media and the polls drive each other loosely. Most of the other candidates show the same general pattern.

We typically see a rise after the candidate announcement, then general agreement with the level of media coverage even though the peaks don't line up. Clinton seems to be the exception: Her popularity seems to have less to do with coverage volume than any other candidate. Maybe that's because we've known for a very long time that she was going to run, and we should really plot this chart back another year or two.

My sense is that what we have here is a feedback loop. Does media attention increase a candidate's standing in the polls? Yes. Does a candidate's standing in the polls increase media attention? Also yes. And everything else which sways both journalists and voters in the same direction just increases the correlation. The media and the public and the candidates are embedded in a system where every part affects every other.

It's all of these forces acting in concert that tend to bind media attention and popularity together. It's not that media attention has no effect—we have good reason to believe it does, both from this data and from other research. It's just that the media is not all powerful, despite what the close correlation suggests.

What Is Fair Election Coverage?

Faced with the awesome ability to influence the outcome of an election just by drawing attention to a candidate, how *should* the media cover an election?

No editor is sitting there saying: *Hey, Cruz gained five points, let's cover him 5 percent more.* But journalists do respond to audience attention. Reporters and editors are driven by lots of different demand signals, such as how many people read yesterday's article about a candidate, or how many people are talking about a candidate on social media or—let's be honest here—how popular someone seems to be based on how much coverage they are getting from other journalists! Some newsrooms even plan coverage based on how many people are searching for a given topic.

The media is regularly criticized for chasing popularity, and in this sense it's true. Bernie Sanders says the "corporate media" trivialize the issues and only care about profits. There is certainly no profit without readers—there's no funding either, if you're a nonprofit newsroom. The rapper Common says "the integrity of the media is gone" when journalists decide "we're going to show Donald Trump because we know it's about numbers." And these complaints are not wrong. I began writing this piece to explore the media's relationship to Trump in part because I knew a piece about Trump was likely to be widely read!

Yet for all the newsroom profit pressure and manic metric checking, journalists don't *only* chase popularity. The American media cover a great many things that few people pay attention to, especially international stories. For example, there was extensive coverage of bombings in Lebanona day before the Paris attacks, despite complaints to the contrary. There's an ongoing, thoughtful conversation among journalists about how to balance what gets clicks with what's important. That is, what *journalists* think is important. I'll say this for writing what the audience wants to read: It's democratic.

So should a candidate get media attention according to how many people want to read about them? On some level, yes. But if you think Trump shouldn't be leading or Sanders should be, this probably doesn't seem fair to you. To the degree that media attention causes a candidate to become more popular, there's a winner-take-all effect here: The leading candidate will get the most coverage, boosting their lead. Meanwhile, the media has the potential to trap a candidate in last place because they can't get the coverage they would need in order to rise in the polls.

But what's the alternative? Should journalists cover every candidate equally? This might make a certain amount of sense in the general election, where we only have two major parties. The FCC still enforces the equal time rule which says that if a radio or TV network gives one candidate airtime, they have to give the same amount to other candidates. But that rule doesn't apply to news programs, and that's probably for the best. It's ridiculous to imagine journalists struggling to reach story quotas, so that each candidate gets the same amount of press.

But if not equal time, should journalists strive for some other redistribution of attention? This would necessarily mean less coverage for the leaders and more for everyone else. This might lead to more competitive elections, in that it would counter the winner-take-all tendency of the current system. But it would also mean intentionally *not* covering Trump as much. This might balance things out in an abstract sort of way, but it would also open the media to charges of censorship—and those charges would not be without merit.

It also won't work to suggest the press should just report "current events" or whatever is "newsworthy," as if the news makes itself. Journalism has become less and less about events over the last 50 years, and more and more about context and analysis. And that's okay: Politicians and brands are their own media channels now. If all you want to know is what a candidate did today, you can just follow them on social media—no need for professional journalists at all. Journalists have to add value in other ways now, such as providing context or digging deeper. There's no obviously "right" number of stories about a candidate.

Somewhere, somehow, professional journalists have to decide who gets covered—and any formula they could choose is going to appear biased to someone. In the end, the candidates who attack the media are right about one thing: The press is a political player in its own right. There's just no way to avoid that when attention is valuable.

13

Was the 2016 US Election an Outlier?

Danielle Kurtzleben

Danielle Kurtzleben is an NPR political reporter at the Washington desk. Her responsibilities include appearing on the show, writing for the web, and serving as a regular contributor on the Politics Podcast. *Kurtzleben specializes in economic policy, gender politics, and demographics.*

The presidential campaign of 2016 was unusual, with many atypical political situations surfacing during the race. Various political strategists were surprised by the actions of then-candidate Donald Trump, and of the electorate that would eventually vote him into office. Numerous political insiders present their perspectives on what took place during the 2016 election, especially the actions and appeals to voters and what surprised them the most. The question many are asking is whether this is a harbinger of elections to come or if it was an outlier. Analysis of the 2016 election may give insight into how to predict and understand elections going forward.

The 2016 presidential campaign feels like a political science dissertation (or 1,000) waiting to happen: two massively unpopular major-party presumptive nominees; a strong challenge for the Democratic nomination from a self-proclaimed "democratic socialist"; and the way that Donald Trump has conducted so much of his campaign via Twitter should provide Ph.D. candidates ample material for decades.

On the eve of the Republican convention, where the GOP is about to nominate Trump its standard-bearer, here are some thoughts we've gathered from people who think about this stuff for a living. Over the past month, we asked a group of political scientists and analysts how 2016 is changing how they think: What conventional wisdom is gone now; what surprised them?

Perhaps unsurprisingly, a lot of these answers revolve around the Trump phenomenon, but others say we may have to rethink what voters want—and how to measure those attitudes. The answers of 10 political thinkers are below. (And, of course, these are their opinions alone; none of them reflect the opinions of NPR.)

These responses have been edited for length and clarity.

Maybe We've Been Measuring Voter Attitudes All Wrong

"I know there's been a big fuss about the validity of *The Party Decides*, but for me, I've been most interested in seeing how Median Voter Theory applies to this election. I don't think anyone thought that Donald Trump would appeal to the median GOP voter, much less the general election voter. But now we have to consider that. This will necessarily prompt how we measure voter attitudes, particularly how we identify the attitudes that influence vote choice."

— *Andra Gillespie, associate professor of political science, Emory University*

Race-Based Appeals Seem to Have Worked

"The obvious answer to this is that Donald Trump's popularity and support have surprised me the most—not because we didn't know white consciousness or white identity or attitudes about race in general were important to people, but because he so explicitly framed his campaign this way—and people still hopped on board.

Some prior work had shown that the way to combat implicit appeals to attitudes about race and ethnicity and identity was to make them plain—sort of the way Jesse Jackson did in 1988 with the ad called "Revolving Door," which many thought contained implicit appeals with white voters' fear of black men. But here, we have a candidate who explicitly and plainly frames his campaign around attitudes about race and ethnicity and it doesn't backfire, it works.

Even more surprising was the way Trump weaved national security into his messaging on race, ethnicity, and identity. It was a surprising messaging package because of its explicit nature. I would have expected to see this played with much more subtlety. I was also shocked that so many people thought this kind of rhetoric was acceptable—even if they hold the same attitudes. I was also a bit surprised that elites within the Republican Party didn't coordinate around one of the other candidates with enough time to keep Trump from the nomination."

— *Lynn Vavreck, professor of political science and communications at UCLA and co-author of* The Gamble

Are "Data Pundits" Getting It Wrong?

"This is a difficult question to answer. As a 'real' scientist, I regard most political science conventional wisdom as having a less secure foundation than natural sciences. In other words, their knowledge is provisional. So if an idea like *The Party Decides* goes down, that is not a total surprise. I am surprised to see 'data pundits' get caught between hard data and conventional wisdom, and then go down the path of conventional wisdom. That shows how hard it is to resist the pull of what others are saying.

I am somewhat surprised to see how little difference there is between Donald Trump's overall pattern of support this year and Mitt Romney's in 2012. For the most part, purple states then are still purple states now. It seems like the Republican Party's base voters are open to a very wide range of candidates. It seems clear that this year, there is no realignment of voters—not yet, anyway.

Conversely, political science is an area where it's nearly impossible to do what I would call a real experiment. Looks like Trump is about to do one for them. In the next four months we are about to see the results of a giant experiment in which we find out how many votes Republicans can get when their candidate doesn't have a real campaign apparatus and has sky-high negative ratings."

— *Sam Wang, writer for the Princeton Election Consortium blog, which keeps a data-based battleground map. (He's also a Princeton molecular biology professor)*

Race and Geography, Not Social Issues, Are Driving Politics

"I want to make a point more generally about party politics: nomination battles in both parties have made me convinced that race and geography are driving features of American party politics, and social-issue divides are less enduring and influential. I had an inkling last year that the urban-rural divide in the Democratic Party didn't get enough attention (after attending the Wisconsin state convention), but few of my colleagues took that idea seriously. Now I think it's pretty apparent."

— *Julia Azari, professor of Political Science, Marquette University*

Celebrity Has Taken Over Washington

"I think the extent to which politics has become celebrity-driven has just been epitomized and reached its logical conclusion in this election cycle. I remember 20-some years ago having some friends in D.C., and they either worked on campaigns or they were just going to school, and they were starting to take pictures with politicians.

Politicians started to feel to me like celebrities. That was like 20 years ago, and I think we've just steadily continued that trend.

And it's obviously epitomized in Donald Trump being the ultimate celebrity politician. The extent to which celebrity is prized in our society and has infiltrated politics is shocking to me. And the extent to which the mistruths and the falsehoods of the Internet have been mainstreamed into American politics....

Things that are very easy to debunk are gaining currency in politics, and we've lost the gatekeeper. We've lost the ability to have rational conversations based on facts, and falsehoods are just not checked. And so I guess that has surprised me that we've gotten to this point. And I think it's not new; I think it's been building. It's just kind of exploded this year."

— *Marty Cohen, professor of political science at James Madison University and co-author of* The Party Decides *(excerpted from NPR's June interview with him)*

Maybe "the Latino Vote" Isn't As Important This Year as Everyone Thought It Would Be

"What [this election] does is it reinforces in a perverse way an argument I've made for a long time, at a time when one would not think—it's been said for many years now that Latinos would influence the presidential election. And this looked like the ideal time, given Trump, his anti-Latino positions, and the argument that Hillary [Clinton] needs Latinos. Well, in fact, it is my expectation that Hillary is really going to stomp Trump. And if I'm right, and I'll bet money that I'm right, Latinos will be absolutely irrelevant in this election.

So there aren't many states where there's enough Latinos, where the margin's going to be so tight that Latinos make a difference. Hillary's going to win California, and Hillary, I don't think, will win Texas—both huge Latino states. And there will be a lot of people voting against Trump, not necessarily for Hillary. And Latinos will be in that group, but that group will be bigger than Latinos."

— *Rodolfo de la Garza, professor of political science, Columbia University*

It's Really, Really Hard to Bust Through Political Conventional Wisdom

"What surprised me the most? The intransigence of conventional wisdom. So many pundits, politicians, 'strategists' and pollsters were heavily invested in the concepts that (1) The party decides, and (2) Trump can't win, that they ignored the resonance and power of Trump's message and the key dynamics of the race itself.

They also failed to understand one of the key elements of 'the party decides' theory—the theory describes what happens when the party actually decides, but it says nothing about what happens when it doesn't. The assumption was that the party always decides. This year it didn't, and Trump was the result on the Republican side.

I expect that conventional wisdom will continue to reign post-November with the media, politicians and others saying (if he is not elected) that Trump was a flash in the pan. My hypothesis is he is not. Trump's authoritarian, ascriptive message is not an anomaly in American history. Its success in 2016, however, is and represents a potentially concerning development for Madisonian democracy (and civil society). Trump's core support is firmly rooted in authoritarianism that, once awakened and stoked, is a force with which to be reckoned. Democracy is about compromise. Authoritarianism is about us-versus-them."

— *Matthew MacWilliams, Ph.D. candidate, University of Massachusetts–Amherst, author of the theory that authoritarianism predicts Trump support*

2016 Is an Outlier, Not a Sign of Things to Come

"This HAS been a strange election. I don't believe the lessons political scientists have learned over the decades should be discarded because of one idiosyncratic presidential election in which many of those lessons don't hold. Perhaps the biggest surprise to me about 2016 is how an unconventional candidate with no political experience captured the nomination of a major political party through the use of celebrity and social media.

Journalists and political scientists have understood the increasing role of social media in modern campaigns; however, the Trump candidacy has demonstrated that a candidate with great name ID and an understanding of social media can parlay that into a great advantage—particularly through earned media and as a way to energize and communicate with supporters. The conventional wisdom among many political scientists—a view I do not share—is that campaigns do not matter; rather, variables such as the economy and presidential approval rating are viewed as the primary determinants of which candidate will be victorious.

The election of 2016, however, is personality-driven—particularly on the Republican side. In a year in which Republicans should have an advantage in capturing the White House after eight years of a Democratic president, the Trump campaign—driven largely by the ramblings and direction of the candidate himself—provides evidence that the candidates and the campaign themselves can impact performance, as measured by polling, and election results, in both the nomination phase and general election. The big question is: is 2016 an outlier or a harbinger of future elections? I think it's an outlier."

— *David B. Cohen, professor of political science, University of Akron*

Trump Created a New Way of Campaigning

"I thought [Trump] would be a flash in the pan. I didn't think a celebrity with as much fallibility and negatives would go so far. Part of the question became, can he turn that fear, that anger, that frustration and in some cases that hatred that many [in his base] were feeling into votes? And he did well enough to win the primaries.

But he did it on a paltry budget. So this whole notion that has been around for a long time in American politics, of money in politics, and that the candidate that has the most typically wins. And even at that, the runner up raises a ton of money too, typically in a major campaign. Well, Trump defied that kind of model that has been existing for many years. He spent very little; he relied on the media and the mainstream media, primarily, that was only too glad to run with virtually any story.

But as well, he didn't have much of an outreach staff in many of the places he was campaigning. And much of the staff that he had, the so-called senior staff, was very inexperienced. So he spun what it means to be a candidate, a competitive candidate, in a national political campaign on its head. Whether that becomes a partial model for someone else down the line remains to be seen. But he is a unique candidate."

— *Jaime Regalado, professor emeritus at California State University Los Angeles*

The GOP Could Have an Easier Shot at the White House

"I'm old enough to have closely followed the 1964 and 1972 presidential campaigns, so I've seen the parties commit suicide before. But in those two years, Presidents Johnson and Nixon were very unlikely to lose, so it wasn't as though a party was throwing away a winnable election. Not so in 2016. With a solid, appealing ticket, Republicans would have had a good shot at retaking the White House. Instead, they nominated an extremely controversial candidate, who appears quite unlikely to win, at least from the perspective of June.

We all know some of the reasons—16 non-Trump candidates split the money and support that could have consolidated behind one of them early on. Along with the rest of us, they didn't take Trump seriously and let him go without withering criticism for much too long. And many news media organizations made a Devil's pact with Trump—loads of endless coverage in exchange for the ratings he brought.

Political scientists have insisted that party leaders decide presidential nominations by means of endorsements, money and other signals of backing. Maybe most of the time that's true. Yet the grass roots of the party can occasionally rebel and conquer the establishment, as Goldwater, McGovern, and most of all, Trump prove. Electability isn't much of a consideration for ideologues—or they convince themselves against the evidence that their own choice is the people's choice."

— *Larry Sabato, professor of political science, University of Virginia*

14

Because of the Media, Too Much Coverage Is Given to Celebrities

Pew Research Center

As a nonpartisan fact tank, the Pew Research Center informs the public about the issues, attitudes, and trends at work in the world. Pew conducts public polling research and does not take positions on policy.

The opinion of the individuals polled by the Pew Research Center is clear: there is simply too much news coverage given to celebrities and their assorted scandals. A much smaller share believes that the public's appetite for celebrity news and scandal drive this news coverage. It is interesting that young people think the public should claim responsibility for their interest in celebrity news and scandals, while older poll participants think the blame falls solely on the media.

An overwhelming majority of the public (87%) says celebrity scandals receive too much news coverage. This criticism generally holds across most major demographic and political groups. Virtually no one thinks there is too little coverage of celebrity scandals.

When asked who is most to blame for the amount of coverage these kinds of stories receive, a majority of the public points to the media. Fully 54% of those who say celebrity news is over-

"Public Blames Media for Too Much Celebrity Coverage," Pew Research Center, August 2, 2007.

covered also believe news organizations are to blame for giving these stories so much coverage. Roughly a third (32%) say the public is to blame for paying so much attention to them, and another 12% say the media and the public are both equally to blame.

Men and women generally agree on this question, although women tend to follow tabloid stories more closely than do men (52% of men and 55% of women blame news organizations for all the coverage). Republicans and Democrats also agree on this issue—though Republicans are often more critical of media practices (57% of Republicans and 52% of Democrats blame the media for too much tabloid news).

One noteworthy difference in opinion on the question of who is to blame for tabloid news coverage can be seen across age groups. Young people blame the public more than the news media. Nearly half of those under age 30 say it's the public's appetite for scandal news that spurs the amount of coverage, 31% say news organizations are to blame. Among those over age 30, large majorities blame the media, while less than 30% blame the public.

Throughout 2007 there has been no shortage of news involving Hollywood celebrities. Paris Hilton's brief but memorable stint in jail became a national news story earlier this summer. During the first week in June, when she was briefly released from jail and then sent back, 4% of the national news was devoted to the story and 12% of the American public said the Hilton saga was the story they were following more closely than any other. Earlier in the year, Anna Nicole Smith's death was an even bigger story. During the two days immediately following Smith's death, nearly a quarter of the news from all sectors (24%) was devoted to this story. Public interest did not match the amount of coverage, and 61% of Americans said the story was being over-covered. Nonetheless, there was a core audience for the story that stuck with it throughout the next few weeks.

The vast majority of coverage of this year's biggest celebrity scandals—namely Anna Nicole Smith's death and Paris Hilton's legal problems—could be seen on cable television news. During those first two days after Smith's death fully half of cable news coverage was devoted to this story, making it by far the most heavily covered story of the week on cable. Similarly, the Paris Hilton story was featured much more prominently on cable TV news than on other sectors. In the week she was released and then sent back to jail, Hilton was the number three story on cable TV. It was the eighth most heavily covered story on network TV news and it didn't make the top ten in the nation's newspapers.

When asked which types of news organizations give celebrity scandals the most coverage, the public points to television but does not make a clear distinction between cable and network TV. Roughly a third (34%) say cable news networks such as CNN, MSNBC and the Fox News channel are the biggest purveyors of celebrity news. Another 27% say that the big three network news outlets give these stories the most coverage. Internet news websites are cited by 15% of the public, 8% name newspapers and 4% point to radio news programs.

Democrats are more likely to say cable news has the most celebrity coverage, as opposed to network news (37% say cable, 25% say network). Republicans are evenly split on the issue (31% cable, 30% network). Young people are among the most likely to list cable as the worst offender—40% of those under age 30 say cable news has the most celebrity coverage, only 17% point to network news.

One of the most recent celebrity scandals, Lindsay Lohan's arrest on a second drunken driving charge, generated little interest from the public. Only 8% followed this story very closely last week, another 19% followed the story fairly closely.

These findings are based on the most recent installment of the weekly *News Interest Index*, an ongoing project of the Pew Research Center for the People & the Press. The index, building on the Center's longstanding research into public attentiveness to major news stories, examines news interest as it relates to the news media's agenda. The weekly survey is conducted in conjunction with The Project for Excellence in Journalism's *News Coverage Index*, which monitors the news reported by major newspaper, television, radio and online news outlets on an ongoing basis. In the most recent week, data relating to news coverage was collected from July 22–27 and survey data measuring public interest in the top news stories of the week was collected July 27-30 from a nationally representative sample of 1,027 adults.

Iraq and Campaign Top News Interests

In the news this week, the public's interests and the news media's agenda were not completely in sync. Interest in the Iraq war remained high, in spite of relatively little coverage of events on the ground. Fully a quarter of the public said the Iraq war was the single news story they followed more closely than any other last week, making it the public's top news story. At the same time the national news media devoted 3% of its overall coverage to the war, making it the sixth most heavily covered news story of the week. The public's sustained interest in the war, even during weeks where the coverage is sparse, highlights the importance Americans place on the story.

The Iraq policy debate received slightly more news coverage last week than events on the ground in Iraq (4% of the newshole). Roughly a quarter of the public paid very close attention to the policy debate and 8% listed it as their most closely followed story of the week.

The 2008 presidential campaign was the most heavily covered news story last week. The majority of the campaign coverage was focused on the Democratic debate sponsored by CNN and YouTube where ordinary citizens submitted questions to the candidates via videotape. Nearly one-in-five Americans followed campaign news very closely and 12% said this was the story they followed most closely.

The second most heavily covered news story of the week involved Attorney General Alberto Gonzales and the controversy surrounding his recent statements to Congress. The national news media devoted 6% of its overall coverage to this story. Public interest in this story remains relatively low, as the focus has expanded from Gonzales's involvement in the firing of eight U.S. attorneys to questions about whether he misled Congress on important national security issues. This past week 15% of the public followed the Gonzales story very closely, unchanged from last month and down slightly from late-March and early-April when 22% were following the story very closely. Republicans and Democrats are following this story in nearly equal proportions—a change from earlier months when Democrats were tracking the story much more closely than Republicans.

The gruesome murders of a mother and her two daughters in Cheshire, Connecticut drew a relatively large news audience last week. Although only 12% said they followed the story very closely, 9% listed this as the story they followed most closely, making it the number three story in terms of news interest. Overall, the national news media devoted 2% of its coverage to this story.

News about last week's stock market plunge was followed very closely by 15% of the public, 7% listed the stock market's recent ups and downs as their most closely followed story. The national media devoted 2% of its overall coverage to stock market news.

Sports Scandals Hit the Front Page

Several sports scandals have become national news stories in recent weeks. The most prominent story involves allegations that NFL quarterback Michael Vick was involved with illegal dog fighting. One-in-five Americans (21%) followed this story very closely, last week another 27% followed it fairly closely. The national news media devoted 2% of its overall coverage to the Vick story.

The controversy surrounding Barry Bonds' baseball career as he comes close to breaking Hank Aaron's career home run record hasn't generated as much news coverage as the Vick allegations, nor is the public as interested in this story (12% followed this story very closely). News about a former NBA referee who is under investigation for betting on games including some he officiated has drawn the very close attention of 9% of the public, another 22% are following that story fairly closely.

Men are following the Vick story more closely than are women (26% vs. 17% very closely). The racial gap on this story is significant with 32% of blacks following very closely compared to 20% of whites. Young men are among the most interested in the Bonds story—22% of men under age 50 are following the story very closely. Blacks and whites are about equally interested news about Bonds.

About the News Interest Index

The *News Interest Index* is a weekly survey conducted by the Pew Research Center for the People & the Press aimed at gauging the public's interest in and reaction to major news events.

This project has been undertaken in conjunction with the Project for Excellence in Journalism's *News Coverage Index*, an ongoing content analysis of the news. The *News Coverage Index* catalogues the news from top news organizations across five major sectors of the media: newspapers, network television, cable television, radio and the internet. Each week (from Sunday through Friday) PEJ will compile this data to identify the top stories for the week. The *News Interest Index* survey will collect data from Friday through Monday to gauge public interest in the most covered stories of the week.

Results for the weekly surveys are based on telephone interviews among a nationwide sample of approximately 1,000 adults, 18 years of age or older, conducted under the direction of ORC (Opinion Research Corporation). For results based on the total sample, one can say with 95% confidence that the error attributable to sampling is plus or minus 3.5 percentage points.

In addition to sampling error, one should bear in mind that question wording and practical difficulties in conducting surveys can introduce error or bias into the findings of opinion polls, and that results based on subgroups will have larger margins of error.

15

Athletes Should Focus on Sports, Not Politics

David French

David French is a senior fellow at the National Review Institute, a veteran of Operation Iraqi Freedom, and a senior writer at the National Review. *French is a lawyer and the author of* Rise of ISIS: A Threat We Can't Ignore.

Should celebrity athletes be able to voice their political opinions or protest during sporting events? Some athletes believe they have every right to do so. However, fans have also reacted to such displays, and in the case of Colin Kaepernick's protests many of them stopped watching the NFL. Will the phenomenon of sports figures becoming political protestors continue, level off, or disappear? Some think it will and should continue, while others contend that the field should be for sports, not for politics. French belongs to the latter camp, asserting that sports should be a respite from political turmoil.

When players get political, it turns out that fans can get political right back. After months of speculation and piles of anecdotal evidence, market-research company J. D. Power has weighed in with real data. After surveying 9,200 fans, researchers found that "national anthem protests were the top reason that NFL fans watched fewer games last season." The protests were never popular. A September 2016 Reuters poll indicated that a super-majority of 72 percent of Americans believed the protests, led by

"Politicize Sports, Pay the Price," by David French, National Review, July 28, 2017. Reprinted by permission.

Colin Kaepernick, were "unpatriotic," but evidence that his protest had an impact on ratings was spotty, at best. Now that's changed.

To be sure, there were a number of other factors that affected viewership, from the pace of the game to off-field domestic-violence incidents, but 26 percent of those who tuned out the NFL did so because of the anthem protests. In spite of the fact that conservative boycott efforts rarely bear fruit (we're better at buycotts, just ask Chick-fil-A), I can't say that I'm surprised. As the Left is learning, the politicization of everything won't always work to its benefit. Two sides can play that game.

It's important to note, however, that it wasn't just the fact of Kaepernick's protest that ignited such a backlash. After all, athlete-led protests are hardly unprecedented. But his was particularly classless, his supporters were spectacularly condescending and arrogant, and he consequently exposed a political rot at the heart of an industry.

Let's not forget that Kaepernick didn't just confine himself to quietly kneeling. For a time, he relished breaking norms and inflaming fans. He wore socks depicting pigs in police hats. He showed up at a press conference in a Fidel Castro T-shirt. And through it all, sportswriters and commentators cheered him on. The elite sportswriting consensus was so much *in favor* of Kaepernick that it became somehow "controversial" to reflect the mainstream American view that kneeling was inappropriate and unpatriotic.

In short, sportswriters who could brilliantly break down the weaknesses of the Cover 2 defense proved that they were no better than dorm-room ideologues when speaking about politics. They knew they were right. Their peers mainly agreed with them. And anyone who disagreed was ignorant and likely racist. In an influential and widely shared piece, *The Ringer*'s Bryan Curtis outlined the level of intolerance:

> Forget the viability of being a Trump-friendly sportswriter today. Could someone even be a Paul Ryan–friendly sportswriter— knocking out their power rankings while tweeting that

Obamacare is a failure and the Iran deal was a giveaway of American sovereignty?

In sportswriting, there was once a social and professional price to pay for being a noisy liberal. Now, there's at least a social price to pay for being a conservative.

The Kaepernick protests thus metastasized from one man's classless protest to saturation-level fawning and hectoring. And when *Paul Ryan* is too radical a figure for members of a profession to support, there is little doubt that the profession has lost its way. With few exceptions, groupthink breeds arrogance and ignorance, not thoughtfulness or insight.

What now? Will players and leagues dial back their activism? Sports leagues have been moving left, even engaging in outright political activism to bully states into dropping expanded protections for religious liberty. ESPN has also steered sharply to port, transforming itself into the MSNBC of sports. Left-wing activists relentlessly argue that athletes should "use their platform" for "social change." In some quarters, it's as if sports is merely a means to an end. A point guard develops a jump shot *so that* he can declare, "Hands up, don't shoot." A linebacker is somehow wasting his gifts if he's not blasting Trump on Twitter.

There are some signs that a message has been received. Colin Kaepernick is still looking for a job, and it's silly to think that public disapproval doesn't play a role. Elite football skills can cover a multitude of sins, but owners can easily swap one mediocre quarterback for another to avoid a public backlash. I would be surprised if the NFL sees another wave of anthem protests this year.

But that doesn't mean all is well. That won't mean sports is getting less political. New issues and causes will arise, and I fully expect to see athletes, coaches, journalists, and even the leagues themselves jump back into activism with both feet. And to the extent that the backlash is seen as explicitly conservative, that will only further inflame the loudest voices on the athletic left.

In reality, only the market can save us now. And that market message has to be clear—keep politics out of sports. That of course doesn't mean that athletes aren't citizens like the rest of us, that they should just "shut up and play." But it does mean that the wholesale conscription of entire leagues and entire professions into the leftist-industrial complex has to end. Athletes conservative and liberal should be equally free to share their views, sportswriters should be as diverse as their audience, and leagues should stay out of the political fray. And, above all, when game day arrives, let's leave the politics at home.

On Sundays, the Trump Train can rest at the station. The #Resistance can take a break. The truly important question this fall is whether Tom Brady is man or cyborg. Can he defy Father Time one more year? Does our yellow sun provide him with inhuman powers? America needs those answers far more than it needs to know the NFL's position on the "compelling governmental interest" test in religious-freedom cases or a backup quarterback's stance on police escalation of force. The field is for sports. Statements are for Twitter. When it comes to politics, athletes and sportswriters should be woke on their own time, not ours.

16

Should Athletes Speak Out?

GLOBSEC

GLOBSEC is an international think tank committed to improving the future by supplying ideas and solutions for a safer world. This organization works to encourage a free exchange of ideas in Europe and throughout the world.

In many ways the 1960s and 1970s were the jumping-off point for athletes as social and political protestors. American and European athletes used their professional sports platforms to demonstrate against injustices that concerned them. Towards the end of the twentieth century, sports became a very different arena: celebrity athletes made big bucks from endorsements and advertising. Because of sponsorships and branding, celebrities could no longer speak out or demonstrate for fear of losing lucrative sponsorship deals. Around 2016, the pendulum began to swing back: sports stars were protesting again.

Considering the harm that doping does to sport, the International Olympic Committee's (IOC) recent decision to ban Russia from the 2018 Winter Olympics but allow clean Russian athletes to compete as an Olympic Athlete from Russia (OAR) can be perceived as objective and impartial. Indeed, despite Moscow's expected discontent with the ban, two icons of Russian ice-hockey—Alexander Ovechkin and Ilya Kovalchuk—clearly

"Should Athletes Speak on Political and Social Issues?" GLOBSEC, August 1, 2018. Reprinted by permission.

expressed their opinion that clean athletes must go and compete. Their influence over fellow athletes wavering over the decision to compete under the OAR banner should not be underestimated.

While top sportsmen commenting on specific social and political issues is nothing new, it nevertheless remains a highly controversial subject. On the one hand, the views of famous athletes can help to raise public interest in many important topics. But there also times when their activities are criticised as having an unhealthy influence over their followers, most notably the young and disaffected.

Origins

The 1960s and 70s are widely regarded as the beginning of sport's active engagement with social and political issues. In 1967, boxing legend Muhammad Ali used his superstar status to openly speak out against poverty, racism and the Vietnam war. The Black Power salute by African American sprinters Tommie Smith and John Carlos has become an iconic moment in sporting history. During their medal ceremony at the 1968 Summer Olympics in Mexico, both athletes raised a black-gloved fist as a sign of protest against racism and poverty in the United States. Their gesture split public opinion over whether it was a sign of courage or disrespect.

Smith and Carlos were not the only athletes to court controversy during a medal ceremony at the 1968 Summer Olympics. Czechoslovak artistic gymnast Věra Čáslavská, the holder of seven Olympic gold medals, turned her head down while the Soviet national anthem was played. Her gesture was a silent protest against the Soviet occupation of Czechoslovakia.

In Retreat

Fast forward to the end of the 20th century and the situation could not have been more different. An athlete's primary interest was to perform to their best and show loyalty to financial donors rather than get involved in politics. One of the most famous athletes avoiding any kind of controversy during this era was basketball player Michael Jordan.

Many leading sportsmen and sportswomen have also shied away from expressing political views in the opening decades of the 21st century. That's because many athletes have obligations towards their commercial sponsors and brands. Binding athletes not to speak on political issues increases the buying potential of the general public by not excluding those with notable differences of opinion.

The material rewards for staying tightlipped on hot-button issues are plain to see. From Brazilian footballer Neymar to Swiss Tennis star Roger Federer, and beyond, sport is awash with athletes whose incomes are higher thanks to marketing and sponsorship rather than sporting prowess. Indeed, the earning potential of many top sport stars has grown in line with increased television coverage, clever scheduling and social media.

Times They Are A Changing?

Which makes protests that have sporadically occurred during National Football League (NFL) matches since August 2016 intriguing. During a preseason game, American football player Colin Kaepernick sat on the bench while the US national anthem was played. This gesture was later transformed into going down on one knee and explained as an attempt to highlight racial injustice and police brutality against African Americans. Since then, more than a hundred players—the vast majority of them African Americans—have joined the protest. US President Donald Trump and some NFL fans have branded the gesture as disrespectful and unpatriotic.

The protests have continued elsewhere. Last September Stephen Curry, a US basketball player and 2017 NBA champion, caused controversy when he declined to visit the White House. The Golden State Warriors player perceived this as an opportunity to voice his disapproval of US President Trump's opinions. Both sets of protests, in turn, reflect that the United States remains divided over the human rights of African-Americans. One side remains determined to right historical wrongs and fight the US's systemic problems with racism and police brutality. This issue is very sensitive and every time there have been efforts to solve it, obstacles appeared.

Elsewhere, FC Barcelona defender Gerard Piqué highlighted his support for Catalan independence during last year's controversial referendum. It was a declaration that made the Spanish international unpopular among some of the national team's supporters. Piqué's response was an offer to retire from international football if his support for Catalan secession is to be an issue.

Athletes are starting to publicly engage with politics again. Going into 2018, it will be fascinating to see how many more will put their name behind specific social and political causes. Each major sporting protest will most likely be met with the age-old argument that politics and sports should always be kept separate. However, sport is so intertwined with many societies' cultures that it is often difficult to keep politics off the playing field. Both sides of the argument need to up their game if they want to break the deadlock.

17

Sports, Like Politics, Should Be a Force for Good

Benjie Goodhart

Benjie Goodhart is a freelance journalist and frequent contributor to the Guardian.

Since when did sports stop serving as a force for good, bringing together people and uniting them around just causes? The great US track star Jesse Owens did just that by winning four gold medals in the 1936 Olympics, thereby smashing Hitler's ridiculous notions that only Aryans were capable of supremacy in all areas. In the past, politicians have supported teams in their effort to unite their countries behind a goal. Sports can and should be a force for good, and the world should take notice.

A recent blog of mine provoked the kind of ire normally reserved for drug dealers, serial killers and Jade Goody. With this in mind, I have decided today to concentrate on life's less emotive issues, namely politics, human rights, genocide and the role of sport.

"Politics and sport make uneasy bedfellows": the phrase is sufficiently ubiquitous to be a cliché. It is also the worst form of moral abjuration, designed to relieve the social responsibilities of players, owners, sponsors, administrators and fans, leaving us free to enjoy sport unfettered by any tedious ethical dimensions.

"Why sport and politics do mix," by Benjie Goodhart, Guardian News and Media Limited, May 18, 2007. Reprinted by permission.

These "uneasy bedfellows" have more in common than either would choose to admit. Both are partisan affairs, veering between indescribably boring and impossibly entertaining, occasionally erupting into violent conflict. They are characterised by large earnings and backhanders in brown envelopes, and can often appear boorish, loutish, testosterone-fuelled, primal, animalistic and competitive. And both frequently involve a load of balls.

Politicians are quick to emphasise their popular credibility by nailing their football colours to the mast. Interestingly, they almost always support uncontroversial, mid-ranking teams who get up nobody's nose. Would John Major, David Mellor and the late Tony Banks have been as keen to flout their Chelsea credentials after the club became so successful and therefore unpopular? Would Gordon Brown confess if actually he followed Celtic or Rangers rather than the slightly less problematic Raith Rovers?

But just as politicians can use football as a political, erm, football, so sport can also be used as a force for political good. This was never more clearly demonstrated than by the great Jesse Owens, whose four gold medals at the 1936 Olympics were a public and eloquent repudiation of Hitler's repugnant assertions of Aryan supremacy. At a stroke, the Nazi ethos was laid bare in all its vainglorious idiocy.

More recently, South Africa's 1995 Rugby World Cup victory, and the iconic moment when Nelson Mandela, resplendent in the once-loathed Springbok colours, presented Francois Pienaar with the trophy, transcended sport and nationalistic chauvinism and became a symbol of hope for a damaged nation. Mandela later wrote: "It was under Francois Pienaar's inspiring leadership that rugby became the pride of the entire county. Francois brought the nation together."

Mandela is one of many who has attributed vast significance to the sporting boycott of South Africa in the downfall of apartheid. If he believes sport can be a force for moral and political good, who are we to argue?

But with power comes responsibility, and sport must therefore look carefully at where it casts its shadow. Which brings me to the quandary that is Beijing. It has been said that bringing the Olympics to Beijing would shine the light of international scrutiny on human rights abuses in China. Yet nearly seven years after the country was awarded the games, little has changed for the better. Indeed, in some instances, the move has been counter-productive.

Detention without charge is still rife, the media is bound by restrictive censorship, the death penalty is used with shaming frequency, and ethnic minorities are largely excluded from the economic miracle. The Olympics have actually been used as a pretext for detention without trial, as undesirables are locked up to ensure there are no displays of dissent next summer. Families have also been forcibly evicted to build Olympic sites. An Amnesty International report two weeks ago was scathing of the current civil rights record in China.

China is also the most important supporter of the Sudanese government, and buys 60 percent of Sudan's oil exports. The Chinese government has exercised its veto to block UN resolutions concerning Darfur, to the delight of the Sudanese government. Meanwhile, at least 200,000 people have been killed, and over 2 million displaced, by the senseless conflict.

And we want to go and hold the games in Beijing? Really? There are those who will tell you that sport in general, and the Olympics in particular, should not be politicised. But back in the real world, the Games have always been politicised (Moscow? Los Angeles? Mexico City?). Besides, one of the key principles of the Olympic Charter is "the preservation of human dignity." Nowhere in it is the coda "Except for Tibetans or Sudanese."

I don't pretend to know whether the eyes of the world turning to Beijing, and the influx of tourism to the country, will generate its own momentum and wash away the stench of totalitarianism and human rights abuse in China. "Boycott" is not always a popular word to bandy about, even when it isn't preceded by the word

"Geoffrey." But shouldn't we at least be discussing it? Don't we all, as sports fans, have a responsibility to at least ask ourselves these questions? Or can we really all just be content to sit back, pour a drink, and cheer on Paula Radcliffe?

Organizations to Contact

The editors have compiled the following list of organizations concerned with the issues debated in this book. The descriptions are derived from materials provided by the organizations. All have publications or information available for interested readers. The list was compiled on the date of publication of the present volume; the information provided here may change. Be aware that many organizations take several weeks or longer to respond to inquiries, so allow as much time as possible.

American Psychological Association (APA)
750 First St. NE
Washington, DC 20002-4242
phone: (800) 374-2721
website: www.apa.org

The American Psychological Association is the leading scientific and professional organization representing psychology in the United States. It aims to advance the creation, communication, and application of psychological knowledge to improve lives.

The Conversation
89 South Street, Suite 202
Boston, MA 02111
website: theconversation.com

The Conversation is a not-for-profit online newsroom dedicated to providing the information necessary for a democracy to function. It provides vetted news from expert sources.

Gallup
901 F Street NW
Washington, DC 20004
phone: (202) 715-3030
website: www.gallup.com

Gallup is a polling organization interested in using data to drive research and to use this specialization to help other organizations and leaders. Its data analytics is put to use in a variety of areas and to support public opinion polling and information.

Global Citizen
594 Broadway, Suite 207
New York, NY, 10012
email: contact@globalcitizen.org
website: www.globalcitizen.org

Global Citizen is an active global online community dedicated to social change. Although the focus of this site is directed toward the issue of poverty, the site also contains articles on athlete activists.

Henry J. Kaiser Family Foundation (KFF)
1330 G Street, NW
Washington, DC 20005
phone: (202) 347-5270
website: www.kff.org

The Kaiser Foundation is a nonprofit organization that specializes in providing facts, analysis, and journalism on health issues. The Foundation focuses on health issues as well as the role the US plays in global health policy.

National Public Radio (NPR)
1111 North Capital Street, NE
Washington, DC 20002
website: www.npr.org

NPR is a nonprofit liberal-leaning media organization. Its mission is to work with public radio stations across the country to sponsor programs that educate and inform the public on a wide variety of topics. NPR maintains an informative website including news about politics.

National Review
19 West 44th Street, Suite 1701
New York, NY 10036
phone: (212) 679-7330
email: letters@nationalreview.com
website: www.nationalreview.com

The *National Review* is a conservative-leaning publication with an informative site providing expert coverage of all things political. Immerse yourself in topics covering politics and policy, the world, elections, the White House and much more.

Pew Research
1615 L Street, NW, Suite 800
Washington, DC 20036
phone: (202) 419-4300
email: info@pewresearch.org.
website: www.pewresearch.org

Pew Research is a nonpartisan fact tank that aims to keep the public informed about relevant trends and issues affecting the world.

Politico
1000 Wilson Blvd., 8th Floor
Arlington, VA 22209
phone: (703) 647-7999
email: info@politicopro.com
website: hwww.politico.com

Politico is an American political journalism company. Its mission is to bring accurate, nonpartisan information to those who want to understand politics, Washington, and government issues around the globe.

RealClearPolitics

website: www.realclearpolitics.com

RealClearPolitics is a Chicago-based political news and polling data aggregator. Its staff aims to provide their readership with articles of clear, insightful news about the policies and issues of the day. Their site includes news from the White House, the campaign trail, Congress, and discussions on CNN, MSNBC, and Fox News.

The State Press

950 South Cady Mall
Tempe, AZ 85287-1502
phone: (480) 965-2292
email: execed.statepress@gmail.com
website: www.statepress.com

The State Press is the student-run, independent news source at Arizona State University. It provides in-depth reporting on a variety of topics, including politics.

Bibliography

Books

Kathryn Cramer Brownell. *Showbiz Politics: Hollywood in American Political Life*. Chapel Hill, NC: The University of North Carolina Press, 2014.

Eric Burns. *The Politics of Fame*. New Brunswick, NJ: Rutgers University Press, 2018.

Nancie Clare. *The Battle for Beverly Hills: A City's Independence and the Birth of Celebrity Politics*. New York, NY: St. Martin's Press, 2018.

Mark Harvey. *Celebrity Influence: Politics, Persuasion, and Issue-Based Advocacy*. Lawrence, KS: University Press of Kansas, 2018.

Gary Indiana. *Schwarzenegger Syndrome: Politics and Celebrity in the Age of Contempt*. New York, NY: W.W. Norton, 2005.

Julie Klam. *The Stars in Our Eyes: The Famous, the Infamous, and Why We Care Way Too Much About Them*. New York, NY: Riverhead Books, 2017.

Keith Olbermann. *Pitchforks and Torches: The Worst of the Worst, from Beck, Bill, and Bush to Palin and Other Posturing Republicans*. Hoboken, NJ: Wiley, 2011.

George Packer. *The Unwinding: An Inner History of the New America*. New York, NY: Farrar, Straus and Giroux, 2013.

Alan Schroeder. *Celebrity-in-Chief: How Show Business Took Over the White House*. Boulder, CO: Westview Press, 2004.

Mike Straka. *Grrr!: Celebrities Are Ruining Our Country—and Other Reasons Why We're in Trouble*. New York, NY: St. Martin's Press, 2007.

Kenneth T. Walsh. *Celebrity in Chief: A History of the Presidents and the Culture of Stardom*. London, England: Routledge, 2016.

Periodicals and Internet Sources

Jeremy Barr, "When Stars Like Taylor Swift Get Political, Do Voters Listen?" the *Hollywood Reporter*, October 10, 2018, https://www.hollywoodreporter.com/news/stars-like-taylor-swift-get-political-do-voters-listen-poll-1150812.

David Blum, "It's the Baldwins, Stupid," *Esquire*, November 1, 1996, https://classic.esquire.com/article/1996/11/1/its-the-baldwins-stupid.

Ronald Brownstein, "Celebrities as Political Activists," AARP, June 30, 2011, https://www.aarp.org/politics-society/advocacy/info-06-2011/NJ-Top-20-Intro.html.

Daniel W. Drezner, "Foreign Policy Goes Glam," the *National Interest*, November 1, 2007, https://nationalinterest.org/article/foreign-policy-goes-glam-1847.

Tricia Escobedo, "How Charitable Are Today's Celebrities?" *CNN Entertainment*, December 17, 2011, https://www.cnn.com/2011/12/16/showbiz/most-charitable-celebrities/index.html.

Allyson Fluke, "Is It Worth Recruiting Celebrities For Your Charity?" *Frontstream*, February 15, 2017, https://www.frontstream.com/recruiting-celebrities-cause/.

Mahita Gajanan, "The Internet is Ready for an Oprah and Tom Hanks White House in 2020," *TIME*, January 7, 2018, http://time.com/5091871/golden-globes-2018-oprah-president/.

Jessica Leber, "Do People Actually Care More When A Celebrity Supports A Charity?" *Fast Company*, August 14, 2014, https://www.fastcompany.com/3034297/do-people-actually-care-more-when-a-celebrity-supports-a-charity.

Tierney Mcafee, "Will Oprah Run for President in 2020?" *People*, January 29, 2018, https://people.com/politics/oprah-run-president-2020-comments/.

Tom Philip, "Alec Baldwin Says He Would Win 'Hands Down' If He Ran For President," *GQ*, June 12, 2018, https://www.gq.com/story/alec-baldwin-says-he-would-win-hands-down-if-he-ran-for-president.

Maria Puente, "Will the Celebrity Factor Matter for Clinton or Trump?" *USA Today*, August 22, 2016, https://www.usatoday.com/story/life/people/2016/08/22/traditional-gop-dem-celebrity-gap-greater-2016-but-does-matter/88420942/.

David K. Randall, "The Truth About Celebrity Giving," *Forbes*, November 24, 2008, https://www.forbes.com/2008/11/24/oprah-philanthropy-celebrity-biz-media-cz_dkr_1124charitycelebs.html#1e006c25dbfd.

Peter Stanford, "Are Celebrities a Help or Hindrance to Charities?" the *Guardian*, June 25, 2011, https://www.fastcompany.com/3034297/do-people-actually-care-more-when-a-celebrity-supports-a-charity.

Katherine Webb, "Does It Actually Help When Celebrities Take On Political Causes?" *Entertainment CheatSheet*, June 12, 2017, https://www.cheatsheet.com/entertainment/does-it-actually-help-when-celebrities-take-on-political-causes.html/.

Index